Robert Winkler Burke of Reno, Nevada, studied evangelical Christianity to explore the differences between existent immaturity and the hope of maturity. He discovered that maturity has its own higher language and surprising outcomes. He describes his work as a magnum opus and a Rosetta Stone—a sword like no other.

Thanks to my dad and mom, Ray and Jimmy Burke, for their ever-lasting support.

Thanks also to Kenyan pastor, Benjamin Wamalwa Khaemba, and cousin Sharon Tomme for spiritual support.

Thanks to the Russian Martial Art Systema's founders, Vladimir Vasiliev and Mikhail Ryabko, as well as their Systema instructors and students.

Thanks to my carpentry mentor, Ray Marten.

And a special thanks to my three sons: Daniel, Christopher, and Jonathan. May their lives be ones in which Godfrey of Ibelin would smile upon, as well as God.

Robert Winkler Burke

Where Do We Go Now, Lord?

A Divine, Comedy Tale of the Christ

Austin Macauley Publishers™
LONDON * CAMBRIDGE * NEW YORK * SHARJAH

Copyright © Robert Winkler Burke 2023

The right of Robert Winkler Burke to be identified as author of this work has been asserted by the author in accordance with sections 77 and 78 of the Copyright, Designs and Patents Act 1988.

All rights reserved. No part of this publication may be reproduced, stored in a retrieval system, or transmitted in any form or by any means, electronic, mechanical, photocopying, recording, or otherwise, without the prior permission of the publishers.

Any person who commits any unauthorised act in relation to this publication may be liable to criminal prosecution and civil claims for damages.

This is a work of fiction. Names, characters, businesses, places, events, locales, and incidents are either the products of the author's imagination or used in a fictitious manner. Any resemblance to actual persons, living or dead, or actual events is purely coincidental.

A CIP catalogue record for this title is available from the British Library.

ISBN 9781035814503 (Paperback)
ISBN 9781035814510 (Hardback)
ISBN 9781035814527 (ePub e-book)

www.austinmacauley.com

First Published 2023
Austin Macauley Publishers Ltd®
1 Canada Square
Canary Wharf
London
E14 5AA

I thank Jade Chen, the artist responsible for the front and back pictures of this book, and I also appreciate the support of her parents, Stephen and Xiaoling Zhou Chen. They operate a wonderful Chinese restaurant in South Reno called 'Chinese Village'. You can reach Jade via email at *jychen.art@gmail.com*

Note to *(Beloved, Ascension-Bound)* Readers,

I, Robert Winkler Burke, of Reno, Nevada USA, studied evangelical Christianity to see differences between existent immaturity and the hope of maturity. I discovered maturity has its own higher language and surprising outcome. Further, I say that certain work I developed is a magnum opus/Rosetta Stone… a sword like no other.

And what, pray tell, is this work? Well, I have made some dowdy internet videos through the years, but they were more for my benefit of putting proper thinking and explanations together, rather than the sake of intended audience of ascension-hungry Padawans in Christ?

But from the videos, along with vast consumption of existent preacher videos on the internet, and also by attending milky chapels mega and minor, I somehow stumbled and bumbled into the high country of God, steak as it were… and as God required of myself and my unusual callings.

What are these callings? Mainly, to explain the paths from milk to meat in Christianity. Therefore, I made what amounts to a thousand points of light for any and all white hat teams (or souls) wishing to go from milk to meat in Christianity. What are these points of light? Poems, mainly. Why poems? Because they can explain 50 pages of a deep chapter of thought in just a page or two. Poetry has always been a higher language of the spirit, mind and being. Higher language is how you access higher territory in God. It is how you go from milk to meat.

Then two years ago, I made a stunning book to explain the poetry and thoughts presented, for free, on my website: *www.inthatdayteachings.com*. This book was kindly published by Austin Macauley Publishers, a hybrid global publishing concern based in London. I am deeply grateful for Austin Macauley's kind patience, professionalism and well wishing. The book is *Think! Like an Advanced Christian*. The sales of this book to date have been disappointing. Was it too early, meaning the audience is *not yet ready* to go from milk to meat? Was it a bad book? God knows.

So Burke decided to make a companion book, one called "Where Do We Go Now, Lord?" But this book would be different. It would be exotically creative. It would have exaggerated story lines. It would be a Divine Comedy. It would copy the style of Mark Twain's Adventures of Huckleberry Finn. It would be written in first person, by an imaginary antagonist to myself.

What is the point of this second book, other than to create a larger readership for both books? Answer: Both books explain how it is that… when a soul is beautified through the excruciation *(death on a cross of ego dying?)* process of overcoming, the indwelling of "Christ-in-You" can be made possible, and when it is made possible… then astonishing, next-realm things happen.

Interested? Then enjoy what I have written wherein I pretend to be not me… not me at all.

Your Author,
Robert Winkler Burke

(What man is a man who does not make the world better?)
(You are not what you are born, but what you have it in yourself to be.)
(If God does not love you, how could you have done all the things you have done?)
– Quotes from the 2005 film Kingdom of Heaven, directed by Ridley Scott

I have no doubt at all the Devil grins,
As seas of ink I spatter.
Ye gods, forgive my "literary" sins –
The other kind don't matter."
– Robert Service

Jeremiah 6:26 – Thus says the LORD, "Stand by the ways and see and ask for the ancient paths, Where the good way is, and walk in it; And you will find rest for our souls. But they said, 'We will not walk in it.'" – New American Standard Bible.

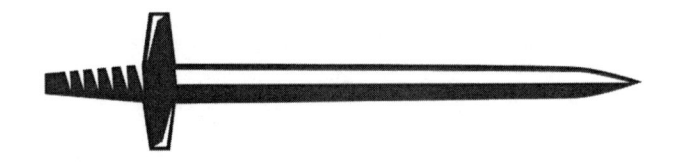

Chapter 1

*W*here do we go now, Lord?

You don't know about me, or what I was trying to do, and how I got into excruciating trouble, and then out of it, and then in it worse and worse… maybe I'm going too deep at the start?

But you don't know about me, unless you have read that book "Think! Like an Advanced Christian" by that man I will show is a liar and a cheat: Robert Winkler Burke.

He lives in Reno, Nevada, that man. And he sure has got nerve, saying *you* or *I* or *anybody* (trained up and called to it) can be an advanced Christian!

Pshaw and fiddlesticks, as they used to say in the old TV Westerns. That book of Mister Burke, well it riled me up something plenty. No way and no how does Jesus return inside of me… or you… or anybody. That's what I said at the end of reading page 174 of Burke's book. No way. No how.

Now, at that time… I wasn't hearing God's voice or anything. Maybe I was hearing the Devil. Maybe not. Maybe I don't really know. But I prayed a prayer. And it went like this.

Father God, I just want to know! I just want to know if you want me to put down this Robert Winkler Burke. Put his reputation down, I mean. And I mean to do it. By whatever means. Will you just let me do that?

In your will, I mean.

Amen in the name of Jesus and the Holy Ghost!

So that's how I started on my journey. My mission of God. Because I am not dumb.

But since this Mister Burke seems to me to be too clever by half… I thought I better make sure I'm smart… So I went on eBay and ordered three computer-robot chess players and set up three games at once, to sharpen my thinking skills before, you know, I attack those crazy, *Jesus-in-You,* Man-of-La-Mancha Windmills of Robert Burke.

Well, that's how I got two fingers broken. How was I to know those robots couldn't tell the difference between my hand on a chess piece and their robot hands moving their chess pieces?

After about two months, I regained the use of my fingers. But they still hurt when I pick my nose when a storm is coming in.

Now I know what you are thinking. Those chess robots and my broken finger were a sign. That Robert Burke said in his book watch out for things like that. That the universe is alive more than we know. That *that* was the Fifth Dimension and beyond percolating. That I didn't have eyes to see nor ears to hear… *what was what.*

No! No! No! I didn't believe in signs. Not then! Nor did anyone else I knew then. Never mind, that's what I always said. *Ha!*

Well, I made those eBay sellers pay! Full refund on those chess bots. And the bad reviews I left! You think they learned a lesson or two from me? *You bet they did.* And praise God, my fingers healed. Only some folks say my right hand is sort of fixed in this "Give-Everybody-the-Bird" way. But I say they are wrong.

So, now that I outsmarted those eBay sellers of robot chess players, and I want to destroy the notion Jesus-in-You really ever happens, and that nobody in real life ever becomes like a Man of La Mancha or Woman of La Mancha, but that it is a sin to think anything like that… and with a million proofs, you dear readers and I, your author, we are going to enjoy… the FULL destruction of the religious notions of Robert Winkler Burke…

So… THEN… after all that! …

Where do we go now, Lord?

Chapter 2

*Y*ou don't know but that I hate hospitals. And doctors. And nurses, even the good looking ones. Well maybe not the *really* good looking ones.

But here I am now in this hospital bed, writing with this Bic pen in my yellow pad journal how I'm going to take down that lofty-headed Robert Winkler Burke and his dumb book "Think Like an Advanced Christian"… which is funny, because I know it would be Christian of me, you know, to please God by taking down the reputation of that book a notch or two! *God, strengthen me to Do Your Will!*

So, anyways, I was at Walmart buying a case of Bic pens and an armful of yellow pads… when I died. I died right there, on aisle 126. Except now I'm alive to tell you about it.

Sudden-Adult-Death-Syndrome, I think it's called. You know: when the person doesn't come back. But I did!

Why did I temporarily kick the bucket? Maybe it's this plate of spaghetti sitting in front of me on the arm attached to the hospital bed, what normally is for dishes of food that patients eat! I ain't eating it, though. *'Cause it's not food!*

What is it, this plate of spaghetti, you ask me, dear reader of the book that proves Robert Burke is wrong? Well, the doctors took it out of my veins. It looks like spaghetti, but it's not. It's way uglier. *Ugly like Robert Burke's sin, I imagine.*

Why was it in my veins? Well, I took four COVID-19 shots and I was triple-masked while in that Walmart stationery aisle. And boy, did I go stationary. *Ha ha! That's a joke.*

What does my enemy, and the enemy of all mankind say about COVID-19? Well on his ridiculous website, called "In That Day Teachings" he has a poem about the vaccine shots where he says, "Wait!" (If you don't believe me you can look it up at www.inthatdayteachings.com.)

Mainly, because of that poem, and because I hate "In That Day Teachings", I took four shots. *I wish I took five.*

When I was dead I met Jesus. We were in a submarine... A US Navy submarine, with nobody on it except me and Jesus, and we were underwater, deep underwater.

"Why are we on a submarine, Jesus?" I asked.

"Because you died, my child," said Jesus.

"If I'm dead, how come I'm still alive?" I asked.

"You are only alive in the afterlife, not on Earth," said Jesus.

"You mean this US Navy sub is on another planet, Jesus?"

"Never mind that, my child, we need to talk."

"Are we on the sub so nobody can hear us?"

"We are on a submarine so you pay attention, and not go off in every direction like a squirrel," said Jesus.

I was *gonna* say what's wrong with squirrels, because you made them didn't you? Except Jesus gave me this look what told me I had better ought to not do that.

Jesus said, "This quest of yours. We in heaven are worried about it. You are trying to discredit Robert Burke because he wrote about Christ-in-You indwelling, and you don't believe it?"

"But Jesus! You're talking to me right now, face to face and you aren't *IN* me. I'm *IN* me, and that's all that's *IN* me. And you are *IN* you. Right, Jesus?" And are you wearing a Navy captain's uniform? And why am I in a sailor's uniform? Shouldn't I be wearing two or three masks over my face?"

Then again, Jesus gave me *that look.*

"Sorry Jesus, I didn't mean to imply you had the "no-symptom" COVID-19 disease and could spread it to me. No, really, I'm fine not wearing a mask with you. Besides, the air in this sub is really great! So fine!"

"Glad you like it, friend," Jesus said. "Now, as for this Quest..."

"Are you going to stop it? Are you *against* me and *for* Robert Burke?" I asked.

"No, my friend, we in heaven all love you both, and everybody on Earth the same, which is more than you could possibly know!"

"Then I can go back to Earth, and you will help me?"

"Correct," Jesus said. "You will have all of my help, and all of heaven's help..."

"To prove Mister Burke wrong?" I asked.

"To see the *TRUTH!*" said Jesus.

Next thing you know, I'm back on Earth in these hospital clothes, the kind with the open back, and I'm on my back, in bed, looking at this plate of spaghetti that's not spaghetti. Only it doesn't *taste* like spaghetti.

Because a man gets hungry waiting to get discharged from the hospital. Too many people got sick who got jabbed, like that was the plan, which I don't believe. And nobody on Earth should either.

I'm just glad Jesus is going to help me! He is my secret weapon, that's what I think!

Chapter 3

*Y*ou don't know... *(Maybe I should stop saying that... Why am I questioning my old habits? I dunno.)* Anyways, you still don't know (ha ha)... *THAT:* before I got home from the hospital, I had *another* adventure, or misadventure you might say.

About the time I'm feeling pretty good even though I'm wearing a shirt that has no back on it... this bossy nurse lady comes in my room and takes the spaghetti-vein plate away and tells me I'm so sick, they have to ventilate me. What she meant, was the doctors, whomever they were... or whomever were the corporate bosses of those doctors were... or whomever DAVOS meeting people demanded those corporate governance bosses who bossed everything down the line... what she meant, was they were gonna give me something called *Remdeseveeer* and put me on a ventilation, breathing con-trapping, I mean, contraption machine.

Well sirs, well madams, as soon as I heard that... something strange inside me happened. *Like it was sin chatting up some plan like normal, but the opposite of that?* I heard as if it were the voice, yes *THAT* voice, the voice of Jesus, who said on the sub: *I was his friend.*

That voice said inside of me, "Norm *(that's my Christian name)* if you let them do that to you, you will die and fail to fulfill your Quest."

And funny thing is... I didn't argue with that voice inside of my head or whatnot. I obeyed it. Because I want to fulfill my Quest!

"Lemee go pee, first!" I said to my Nurse Ratched.

So she let me get off my bed and go to the bathroom in my room. And I grabbed my smartphone. Nurse Ratched didn't notice of that.

Then, well then... this Christian lied. Yup, I lied, big time.

I said, "Don't you know this bathroom toilet is broke and floods the floor everywhere?"

The nurse said she didn't. So she walked me down the hall to the public bathroom. And that's when I bolted. I run. And I kept running, until I was out of the hospital. And I called an Uber. And the driver gave me two masks to wear even though I asked for three. And that's how I got home, alive.

That voice of warning I heard? Was that a Jesus-in-You thing? I say, no… no it wasn't. Couldn't be.

Except… ever since then… I have a yellow folder at my desk I fill with printouts of stories of how so many have died of *Remdeseveeer* combined with ventilators. But who knows the truth about COVID-19 and global eugenics plans since Progressivism was thunk up at the end of the 1800s? Who knows? Huh? Not Robert Burke, nor his book, nor his website, as my Quest will prove.

Chapter 4

*M*y cell phone rang. You don't know it… but my cell phone rang. I was at home, so I rushed to pick it up.

"Where is my cellphone?" I thought.

"UNDER the couch pillow," something told me in my head.

Normally, I don't hear answers like that, so I wondered what was new in my head, except the *Tile-and-All* I was taking… 'cause I was sore from all that hospital running.

"Hello," I said.

Then, like this angel-voice… this kind-a nice lady-voice said…

"Hi! This is Gina, can you hear me?"

"I sure can, Gina!"

(I felt like saying *"Wazzup?… Woman!"* but that would too personal, you know?)

"Glad you can hear me. Know why I had to call you?"

"No, no Gina! Why did you call me?"

Already, I'm liking this lady. She is my friend. Like she is my *INSTA-FRIEND!* Good things are now happening to me! Like percolating coffee!

"SHE IS NOT YOUR FRIEND, NORM. SHE IS A RECORDING," that same voice inside me said.

Gina went on, "I am calling you because of your credit card debt. Would you like to get rid of it, for a small fee? I can transfer you to an agent."

"Gina, are you a real person?" I asked.

There was a pause. Like somebody was gonna punch up an answer for that, that Gina had previously recorded. *(Why was I now being more wise and skeptical? I dunno.)*

20

"Of course, of course! I am a real person!" Gina said. "Let me transfer you to an agent who will reduce your credit card debt for a small fee on your credit card."

Then I got bold. Something in me (normally not EVER in me, at least not normally this quick in me... but instead later I think about what I *could'a, should'a* said.)

I said, "I think you're not a lady. You are a robot or a recording of a robot or a recording of a lady... And I think you are trying to fool me, whoever you are that is punching up recordings of Gina. That's what I..."

But I got interrupted. A man with an Indian or something like Far East accent came on the line, and I could hear it was a crowded call center, with other *India-Stani* guys on the line.

"Your name is Norm, correct?" the man said.

"How'd you know that?"

'We would like to reduce your credit card debt for a small fee. What is your credit card number?"

"HANG UP," said the voice in me.

Well, sirs and madams reading of this book proving Robert Burke is wrong about Christ-in-You and everything else...

Well, this time I didn't argue with that voice. I didn't go off on a squirrel trip on different subjects... You know, *cuttin' and dodging.* Nope. I just... hung up.

And boy, do I feel strange!

Very strange.

Still got my credit card debt, but at least I didn't add to it, like before. (Gotta admit. I've had *lots of befores,* if you know what I mean.)

Honestly, *somethings* in me are telling me to be very, very afraid of this *new voice* inside of me.

I feel strange.

Chapter 5

*Y*ou don't know but it is time for me to visit a preacher I know... in order that we figure a plan to stop that evil Robert Burke and his book and website. God knows, he might even have a YouTube channel!

"You can go in Pastor Far Reach's office now, Mr. Stairmaster."

"It's Starmaster, Becky. Star like a star, not like a stair," I said.

Becky was the pastor's secretary. *(And easy-on-the-eyes, too!)* I didn't mind her getting my name wrong. We was at the *Life is Life, Really-Really Church.* In the offices.

"Sorry, Mr. Norman. He can see you now," she said.

"And *HOW* can I help *YOU* be *SAVED*, Mr. Stair... err... Mr. Starmaster, is it?" said Pastor Far Reach.

Pastor Reach had this habit of preaching in sing-song. I had not really met him in person, this being the first time. And I thought surely he would not talk to me in sing-song. But he did. I thought to myself, I better NOT let myself be mesmerized... like I did at the late Sunday morning service... so that I could capture that feeling of being sleepy and drive home slowly and get to my bed and take a LONG, LONG afternoon nap... as was my custom. No sir! I'd have to keep shaking my head, and blinking my eyes, and even slapping my own face... so as to not get sleepy or drowsy or otherwise completely catatonic!

"Really? *REALLY* now? Of that, *WHO*... is... SURE? And that's why you are here? *HOW*... can... you... be... *SAVED*?

Except he pronounced it "SAVE-ED" ... like a fellow named ED... he was saying. This preacher really butchered pronouncing words... especially if it was

Diety. You know... JEEEEEEE-ZUSSSS... and GO-ODD for God and GAAAAHHWWDD for a different God and such.

"No, Pastor, I'm already saved. I wanna talk to you about this Robert Burke and his book, *Think Like an Advanced Christian.*"

"Pshaw! What a title. Is he saved? This Burke?" he asked.

"No, he is not. He is a sinner and wrong about everything."

"Well, of *COURSE*... he... *IS!* But... *LET* us... *SEE* if... *YOU* are... *SAV-V-V-ED!*"

"Pastor, never mind about me... I..."

"NEVERMIND? Why, do you know there are 800 pages in the Bible?"

"Yes."

"And every page is dedicated to Salvation?"

"What? No."

"*WRONG!* And every verse is dedicated to Salvation?"

"Not every verse, Pastor."

"*WRONG!* And every word in the Word is dedicated to Salvation?"

"There's no way it could be, Pastor Far Reach! What?"

"*WRONG!* Every letter of Every word of Every sentence of Every verse of the Bible is about Salvation! Ess, Aye, El, Vee, Aye, Tee, Eye, Oh, Inn!"

"You don't have to spell it out."

"SALVATION is the thing! It is the *ONLY* thing!"

I didn't know what to say. I just had a blank look on my face.

Pastor Reach then leaned over his desk, and pushed the intercom button to his secretary.

"What is the *ONLY* thing here at this Life is Life, Really-Really Church!!!? Huh, Betty? What is... *THE*... *ONLY*... *THING?*" *pastor yelled into his intercom.*

"Salvation, Pastor Reach," squawked back Betty on the intercom.

"Damn right, Betty. Err... pardon the French!" said pastor.

"I don't mind the French! I kind of like it, Far. Tee-hee," said Betty.

Why was Betty calling Pastor Reach by his first name? I dunno. And pastor now looked... different?

"Uh-HUM. Where were we?" Pastor Reach asked me.

"I'm concerned about Robert Burke and his bad book and website and ideas," I said.

"Well, what does *HE* think?"

"He thinks Christians should grow up, be mature and receive Christ-in-You indwelling, however *that* is possible, which I don't even know about?"

"Claptrap, if he's not focused on salvation!" said pastor.

"And he says Christ-in-You makes you congruent at the proper levels with all that's good, while at the same time making you dissonant or disconnected against all that's bad at proper levels."

"What?"

"He says he wants maturity… or God wants maturity… in us! In seminaries! Churches!"

"Look. I'm busy. The most busy man in the state. Look at what we have!"

"What do you have, pastor?"

"Isn't it obvious? We built a *VILLAGE* on salvation! A little church. A big church. A *GYMNATORIUM!* A school. And the *BIGGEST* church parking lot in the state!"

Then pastor paused for a while. Like he needed to get his puffery down, or get un-puffed somehow.

"AND… What does this Burke have? Hmmm? *(He paused some more.)* A church?"

"No."

"A village?"

"No."

"A parking lot?"

"No."

"Then, forget this Burke fellow. It's *YOU,* God is worried about. I'm worried about *YOU, TOO!* Everybody should be worried about *YOU!* Be SA-A-A-Ave…ED! Or else!"

I said, "Good day, Pastor Far Reach. You're making me defend the man I hate the most on Earth."

Again, the pastor paused. For a long while. We was just eyeballing each other, in a weird way.

"Me?" he asked.

"No, Robert Winkler Burke."

"Well, don't go just yet."

"I'm leaving," I said.

"Well, let me walk you to your car."

"Goodbye, Betty," I said walking out the office with Pastor Reach running after me.

"Bye, Mr. Stairmaster," she said.

"Star-master."

"Here, don't leave in a rush," said Pastor Reach.

He kept after me like that until I got to my car, paying him no mind, and I got in.

"Let go of my car door, Mr. Far," I said.

"*SALVATION*, Mr. Stair! It's all and only about *SALVATION*, Mr. Stair. Don't leave confused. You need to know *SALVATION IS THE ONLY-EVERYTHING,*" he said.

As I drove off… in my rearview mirror I saw Pastor Far Reach, standing in the parking lot with both hands up, all his Village Buildings and his body getting smaller, and smaller and smaller… as he kept yelling… about the only-everything…

"SALVATION! SALVATION! SALVATION!"

Folks, when I got home I felt sick. Sick, like I gotta throw up kind of sick. Like I just ate some really, really bad food. Why?

What is happening to me?

Chapter 6

*Y*ou don't know, but it but I grew up with a preacher's kid who lived down the block – William Reverent the Second. We was pretty good buddies, back then.

But God, how we used to make fun of him when we was kids. His daddy was a preacher with a storefront church, but his mom was a stripper. Yah, I know… I dunno how that worked… except somebody made a country song about it that sold pretty good.

"*Willie!*"

"*Norman!* How good of you to visit my diocese! Do you want to become a Catholic? And do you really think we would have you?"

"What?" I said.

"Just kidding, my old friend from childhood. Turnabout is fair play, or am I wrong?"

"I can't really remember you being wrong. What do I call you… Father? Bishop? William?" I said.

"Friend. Willie. Anything but the Police! *Heh heh.* What has made you darken the doors of this Catholic enclave?" said Reverent.

"Uhm… Well… Uhm… There's this Antichrist author. His name is Robert Winkler Burke," I said.

"I know of him."

"And he wrote a book called *Think Like an Advanced Christian.*"

"Read it."

"And his ideas on his *In That Day Teachings* website are just crazy-bad."

"Poems. You believe his poems are bad?"

"Yes!"

"Well, there is no accounting for taste."

"How come you, a Catholic Bishop, know all this about my sworn enemy? 'Cause Robert Burke kinda writes for the whole Protestant-Evangelical arena, not orthodoxy and Catholics?"

"Norm, Norm, Norman! Was not the Centurion of the New Testament aware of both the traditional Jews and their temples, and also this wondering, radical new revelator, Jesus?"

"Well, of course."

"Then, I am glad, old friend, you also have such on your radar. Bravo."

"Only, I hate him, and his teachings," I said.

"Oh… Shall we take a vow to not eat until he is dead?" said Reverent.

"Come on, Willie! Stop pulling my leg. We're not in Sixth Grade!" I said.

"Seems like…"

"Do you even know how to act like a Father? *For Christ's sake!*" I said.

"Sorry, I'll try to do better, Norman."

"Maybe I should tell you I'm sorry I made fun of you and your parents."

"How long has it been since your last confession, my son?"

"STOP IT! You're making fun of me," I said.

"Mom and Dad are in heaven, now. They always loved you. I never knew why, as you were just a thorn in my side when we were kids. But now I'm beginning to suspect… maybe Mom and Dad were right about you."

"Well, what are we going to do about this Robert Winkler Burke? He is ruining Christianity!" I said.

"Ah, there's the rub! Has he really ruined Christianity? Or has he really ruined one Norman Starmaster?" said Reverent.

"BOTH. Definitely both," I said.

"Friend, if what he is doing is of God, could you ever possibly stop it?"

"No, Willie. I guess not."

"But if what he is doing is NOT of God, do you… *DO YOU…* need to stop it?"

"Well, that's what I don't know. You're about as helpful as Pastor Far Reach. I visited him."

"I shall pray he recovers from your visit."

"There you go again, Willie, making those snide remarks coming from the OPPOSITE way a Man of God should think!" I said.

"And how should we think, in regards to High Teachings?"

"That they DON'T exist. That they CANNOT exist. That they NEVER will exist. Can we pray about it?" I asked.

"Alright, my dear childhood friend, Norman Starmaster. *(Reverent began to pray.)* Heavenly Father, Show us the Truth. And help us to not go mad. In the names of the Father, Son and Holy Spirit. Amen."

"What? Isn't that too short? I expected a *LOT MORE* of you as a Catholic Bishop with all the *FINERY* and all," I said.

"Norman, make the sign of the cross on your chest… Like I just did," he said.

(I did. Even though I am not Catholic. But I did.)

"Goodbye, I guess?" I said.

"Goodbye, Willie. You know, discretion is the better part of valor. I know some things. Seems to me, you are learning some things. Goodbye, Norman. Live up to your *full* name, for once, okay?"

I didn't give him the satisfaction of an answer, his mom being a Go-Go Dancer and all. *The NERVE of some people's children! The NERVE!*

So I went home again, and I thought… *which* man of God was more confusing to me?

And when I finally got to sleep that night, I had no answer, nor when I woke up in the morning. I had no answer at all.

Chapter 7

*Y*ou don't know it but I dream. Not like a regular dream: on a bus, in a car, at home. Nothing like that.

I dream I am watching a play between two people who love each other very much. A twelve-year-old girl called Pringipisa, and her very wise, very great, very martial uncle whom she calls Tio Tio.

The setting is usually the 1600s in Venice, at the uncle's large mansion. Except this is in some great space future, in some other great galaxy, in some other way entirely. Tio Tio is the mentor. Pringipisa is the student.

"How many books are in your library, Tio Tio?"

"Almost enough, my little Princess Pringipisa."

"How shall I ever read them, Uncle?"

"One at a time, child."

"Oh, I love you Uncle! And I always shall."

"No, not always will you. Though our love for each other is great, and for eternity… by the turning of the worlds… soon you will grow into womanhood, your emotions will grow strong, you will want to find a man to marry and boss around like a fish wife does, and you will, on many days, hate me – your poor, old uncle."

"Tio Tio! How can you say such a thing! I shall always love you, and every night I pray I meet a man like you, who will love me, and marry me, and I pray he loves you like I do!"

"How bold of you to argue with your teacher," said Tio Tio.

"I will not be a fish wife! Have you not taught me the sword? I will not become a bossy old woman. Have you not taught me that Earth-book, *Sun Tzu?*

I will not let emotions get the best of me. Have you not taught me high teachings of the Father, Son and Spirit?"

"This great teacher you speak of, Pringipisa. Who is this man? Does he even exist? If he does, I shall use my spaceship and go on a quest to find him! Where is he?"

"He is you, Tio Tio," said Pringipisa.

"No my child, I know the ways of deceivers. I must have inadvertently used these dark ways on you. Do not follow me. Do not marry a poor man of war like me."

"What if I disobey you, and I do?" she asked.

"You will not be the first disobedient child," he said.

"I cannot be a simple, empty-headed schoolgirl. And I will not marry a simple, empty-headed schoolboy become a mere man."

"Oh dear. It appears I have made your life a difficult one, Little One."

"Perhaps, sweet, old Tio Tio. But you have made it an interesting one!"

"I've seen planets crack, solar systems made desolate by civil war. I've seen innocent people hung on a cross… and I don't know why God has given me so much beauty of spirit, soul and body to behold in you, my fiery niece, Pringipisa," said Tio Tio.

"Let's have dinner on the balcony, and the stars will come out, and maybe you can teach me another thing from The Books Which Are Forbidden."

"As you wish, Pringipisa. As you wish."

They dined and enjoyed the setting suns. After the stars came out to boast, the old man of war found a book from his vast library, then found a page in the book, and slowly began to read the following out loud to Pringipisa.

How to Turn a Page (into Knight!)

Book #4 of The Books Which Are Forbidden
Mathew 24:28

Page, wouldst thou become a knight?
Then read herein what I do write,
Thou hast been forgiven *many* mistakes,
Now you shan't. Each one you make,
Will be remembered by me, your mentor,
Become your inquisitor tormentor.

And why remember each new sin?
To spur true repentance deep within,
To oust evil spirits you've long had,
Hiding under grace given when bad,
Now the opposite rule for you applies,
As foul, fey control within you dies.

I shall NOT with you forgive and forget,
God and I love you too much for that,
But if you insist on being brazen immature,
You won't be called out, you'll stay impure.
The choice is thine own now page,
Who art thou, son: knave or sage?

Then the dream ends and I wake up. And I am mad at God.

How come I never had a wise uncle like *that* to mentor me? When I grew up I had big emotions like love, but also rejection and anger and fear. None of it managed. Just problems.

I guess I'm still like that today, even though I'm beginning to feel different. Way different.

Chapter 8

*A*nd I dreamed again…

"Tio Tio, How did you become a Warrior of Faith?"

"You've heard the story, my child… many, many times…"

"I want to hear it again."

"As a young and stupid man, a great one… a great man came to me and told me I have a very high calling as a Man of War."

"And you knew what that was?" asked Pringipisa.

"Do you, my child?" asked Tio Tio.

"I think I do, Tio Tio."

"Then you tell me the story."

"The great one, this man. He was godly?" asked Pringipisa.

"He was."

"He was a warrior of faith?" asked Pringipisa.

"He was."

"He said he would train you?"

"No, he said it was impossible for him to train me."

"Was he wrong?" asked Pringipisa.

"No.

"Why cound't he train you?"

"He wasn't strong enough to crack-down my big, young man ego," said Tio Tio.

"Who did?"

"The Universe."

"The Universe?"

"Yes, Pringipisa. The Universe wins when it comes to the ego fighting it."

"Do I have a big ego, Tio Tio?"

"You have a big will, Little One."

"My will is my ego?"

"At first, yes."

"Will the Universe crack my ego?"

"If you are lucky, you will let it. You will let the Universe win. And be glad of it," said Tio Tio.

"I thought Warriors of Faith win," said Pringipisa.

"First, all great warriors must learn how to lose. If you lose the right way, you always win."

"How do I lose?"

"With kindness. Whether you are to win victorious or lose terribly, always first and foremost be kind."

"Kind?"

"Whether changing a baby's diaper, or patching a wounded enemy, putting down a rogue robot, or cutting flesh with sword… remain human, remain kind."

"Tio Tio, if I was a grown woman, and someone or somethings hurt you… I would come after them and the last thing I would be is kind. That would be the last thing!"

"My dear Pringipisa, again we are at loggerheads. Let us refer to the Books Which Are Forbidden." (Tio Tio walked to his library and picked out a dusty, old book.)

"Okay, Tio Tio… How can you be kind to people who hurt you?"

"When you realize there is a way above the common way. And this way is the undiscovered higher way. Shall I read?" asked Tio Tio.

"Now I feel more like SWORD practice. But (she let go a big sigh) go ahead."

"In that case, then you read," said Tio Tio. (And he handed her a book.)

No One Will Wail

Book #4 of The Books Which Are Forbidden
(Redacted in spirit from the Earth story of Tom Horn, Government Scout and Interpreter)

I'm in jail,
        About to be hanged,
I mutters to God,
        Well, I'll be danged!

I came into town,
        And Sheriff John Brown,
Says, Be my gun hand,
        Son: *Stick around.*

But before I knows it the crazy stage,
        Comes in *too damn fast!*
It's got no passengers, but that driver's,
        Wild drunk off his ass.

No one sees little Emma,
        Two-year-old daughter of John Sheriff,
Toddles into stage's path,
        Too young, dumb, unaware to fear it!

Like thunderbolt, I mounts up,
        From saddle leans down low,
An' up-snatches little Emma,
        Saving! (from mortal blow!)

STOP! You BR-R-R-RUTE!
        Yells uh lady nearby,
Give us the B-A-A-A-BY,
        That baby won't die!

AR-R-R-REST him, Sher-r-r-riff!!
>Is what she said,

He arrested me,
>Now I'm 'bout dead.

That stage coach driver,
>Wouldn't admit: he speeded,

He needed his job,
>And he kept what he needed.

The gentle-ladies agreed,
>*I had planned to steal the baby?*

Saying their good instincts,
>Saved Emma's life, not maybe!

They think: I'm like Black Bart,
>The worst of the bad men I know,

Who has threatened to kill Emma,
>The Sheriff and his wife, Lou Jo!

And in truth,
>*THAT'S WHY I'M HERE,*

To stop Bart,
>'Fore his killin's near!

I heard Bart's plan,
>That he's comin' tomorrow night,

As the *evil-most* man,
>And kill three Browns with knife!

But they'll hang me tomorrow at sunrise,
>And bury me by full-sun noon,

I'll be six feet down, cold like winter,
>When the Browns meet doom.

I could stop Bart easy enough,
> It's what I was born to do,

Good wolves stop *bad* wolves,
> If sheep trust what is true.

But the Sheriff doesn't believe me,
> Thinking I made up Bart's nefarious plan,

I'd like to bust out and kill Bart,
> But I don't have to prove I'm a good man.

Maybe the Sheriff'll make a lucky mistake,
> And I can break out of 'is jail,

Or maybe I'll hang: black-hooded awake,
> *And no one*, no one will wail.

The problem ain't me,
> This town ain't got eyes to see!

I can't fix them,
> They ain't set for any eternity!

Hell, I could go even tonight,
> Or tomorrow at dawn's sun,

I've lived a full life: alright,
> This town ain't even begun.

Maybe I gotta die, *hoo!*
> For the town folk to hate lies,

Maybe the Browns too,
> For raw truth's late surmise.

I've seen plenty of dyin',
> In my life's day,

Dyin', livin' don't matter,
> *Truth* is the way.

Truth must win, yup: it must win,
>And truth must last,
By my example: *for somethin'*,
>To TRUTH, stand fast.

Live or die, or being,
>Rich or poor,
What matters most is,
>Truth is more.

What are these dreams about? I feel like they are saying something to my inner spirit, but danged if I know what they are saying to my head.

I was raised up where everybody said, "Who cares. So what. Nothing matters."

They all couldn't be wrong, could they?

Chapter 9

*A*nd I dreamed again…

"Do you believe in dragons, Tio Tio?"//
"What now, Little One?"//
"Do you believe in dragons?"//
"Only in the kind that live in un-ascended souls. They are very dangerous."//
"Aren't monsters in space more dangerous?"//
"Nothing is more dangerous than the monsters who live in un-ascended souls granted great power and money."//
"Who has great power and money?"//
"Normally the universe – or God – grants power and money to the worthy. The tested."//
"Who are the worthy, Tio Tio?"//
"The ascended."//
"Am I ascended?"//
"Well, you are getting a good start!"//
"Why are dragons in the souls of the un-ascended who have great power and money?"//
"Because an old Earth expression explained it this way: *Power corrupts and absolute power corrupts absolutely.*"//
"Who, in the universe, ever gets absolute power? I mean, besides God?"//
"Well, many have tried and many have succeeded… to their own demise. But not before they almost destroy their planets completely."//
"How can I recognize corrupted planets, run by corrupted leaders?"//
"That, Pringipisa, is the easiest question you have ever asked!"

"How to tell when a whole planet is corrupted by corrupted leaders? How?"

"By the money system."

"What money system?"

"Dear Pringipisa. What is hanging around your neck?"

"A gold cross, on a gold chain. You gave it to me."

"Yes, it is from Earth. What is gold?"

"Gold is gold. No one can make it."

"Where is it found?"

"Everywhere in the Universe, evenly distributed. Scientists say it is made when stars are born."

"Yet, is it rare?"

"Precious, so rare."

"And THIS is OUR galaxy's money system?"

"I thought it was every galaxy's system... of money."

"No. Look at the sad history of Earth. Men of genius intellect used their gifts of mind to create a global debt system made of fiat currency."

"What is fiat?"

"Fiat is by the great power of some nobody... by the empty power of their say-so, a thing has supposed value, while other valuable things... supposedly don't. Evil is good, good is evil. Like that. Good people are pogromed to death. Bad people exalted as gods. That's how you know."

"Know what, Tio Tio?"

"A gold standard for money is how you know if a planet of people are ascended, and not playing God, not playing Big Fish Boss in the Little People Ponds of Slavery... Slavery by the power of the Big Fish People's empty power of their say-so. In short, the people of a planet are forced to believe morals are relative, and to live with the tyrant's boot on their faces, forever... no complaints. It's all a magician's... or a mesmerizer's trick!"

"How will I know a planet is ruled by bad?"

"It will be quarantined, and no space travelers are allowed to visit, or share wisdom... until *that* planet's people fix themselves."

"But if the people of a planet are crushed by debt and meaningless fiat money to toil for... how do they ever get out of slavery?"

"Well, some people with good-God power cheat a little bit and help them. Some people like us, if we... and they... are lucky, by God!"

"By prayer?"

"Huh-uhm. Yes, by prayer and somethings, certain things… beyond that."

"This is hard to understand."

"It's not too hard. It's pretty simple, Princess."

"That's what you always say. I wish we had just *REAL* dragons to fight. That would be better."

"Would it?"

"Then, knights in shining armor would be real!"

"Would they?"

"Are there any knights in shining armor, Tio"?

"Yes."

"Who are they?"

"You, Pringipisa. And everybody like you, trained like you, with a spirit like you."

"Not yet am I! Doesn't feel *ANYTHING* like!"

"How many books in my library have you read?"

"Most. I lost count."

"Sufficient for the task."

"What task?"

"Sufficient to understand a very, very special poem. I will now read it to you. From *The Books Which Are Forbidden*."

"Is it about dragons?"

"Yes."

"Real dragons?"

"As real, and as dangerous… as you ever will encounter!"

"What makes them so dangerous?"

"Their faith that they are right when they are wrong. Their faith they can see when they are blind. Their faith they can hear when they are deaf. Their faith they are mature, when they are babies. And mostly, their faith they are pleasing God when they use the government, or their deceived friends… to kill ascended ones."

"You mean they establish themselves and their worlds entirely on the idea wrong is right, and evil is good, and evil must destroy good… because good is not like themselves?"

"Now you are wise beyond your years, my beloved Pringipisa. This poem unlocked a mystery of two or three thousand years on Earth. The un-ascended could not figure out the Book of Job, a book in the Earth Bible. Now I will read you the poem…"

Fighting Leviathan, With a Puny Wooden Sword!

Book #8 of The Books Which Are Forbidden

Notes from Nelson's Quick Reference Bible Dictionary:
"The book of Job is not only one of the most remarkable in the Bible, but in literature. As was said of Goliath's sword, 'There is none like it,' none in ancient or in modern literature." – Kitto. "A book which will one day, perhaps, be seen towering up alone far above all the poetry of the world." – J. A. Froude. Nelson's comments say that the true identity of who wrote Job has remained throughout time: a mystery.

"Do not break the person, break his desire to attack you. Provide the illusion that your opponent still has control, but make sure he does not." – Mikhail Ryabko, Russian Martial Art Systema Master

"When hitting someone (or changing a baby's diaper) ... remain human." – Vladimir Vasiliev

Joseph Campbell explained the Hero's Journey. It is Job's story and other saints.

I must not hurt huge Leviathan,
    As it swoops down on me!
Dragon's flame kills and maims,
    I'll soon be history!

Oh, woe is me! Oh, woe is me!
    I have but a wooden sword!
From the cross, that victory tree,
    Of Christ, my humble Lord!

Yet, I must not hurt Leviathan,
    Its skin is tough and brittle!
His pride is ridiculous big,
    And I am less than little!
We fight for hours,

    Oh, we fight for days on end!
Then, when it's over,
    The beast gets up again!

My puny wooden sword damages it not,
    I'm like a grasshopper against a giant!
Then it lays down, coughs up its heart,
    Upon its tongue, now on me: reliant!

Leviathan now relies on me,
    To treat its heart with care!
No longer enemies, but fast friends,
    I approach on God's dare!

Oh, woe is me! Oh, woe is me!
    I have but a wooden sword!
From the cross, that victory tree,
    Of Christ, my humble Lord!

With my too-small wooden sword,
    I walk into the danger zone, such biting teeth of dread!
To the heart, now on the tongue,
    I gently touch my sword, out gush bright drops of red!

From the sword come good drops,
    Of God's ancient-wisdom self-sacrifice,
Then Beast wakes up changed,
    Swallows heart and renews its old vice!

Cruelly taking advantage of my nearness,
    Leviathan scorches me in full-blown rage!
I fight him off again with wooden sword,
    Behold! Beast doth weaken! says my Page.

For my Page greatly knows what's going on,
    Not long ago, *HE* was *THE* bad Leviathan!

You see, we fought for years! *Way too long!*
    His dual was an excruciating marathon!

But after a thousand drops from God's cross,
    My Page was, of Beast, set free!
Now he's learning to be God's Man-of-War,
    Who fights evil, *just like me!*

Oh, woe is me! Oh, woe is me!
    I have but a wooden sword!
From the cross, that victory tree,
    Of Christ, my humble Lord!

After days and months and years,
    My Page and I have succeeded!
Leviathan whom we fought,
    Is full humble now: defeated!

My Page has become a Swordsman,
    That Leviathan: HIS own Page,
I have left off sword for pen,
    That you understand this age!

So then, pride of religion and its blinding selfish-rigidness,
    Is killing man!
Just as loving kindness, humility, patience and flexibility,
    Kills Leviathan!

Job learned this In That Day,
    Of his: long ago!
Now we must all learn the same!
    You do not know?

Holy flexibility,
    Is where Christ-in-You is at!
You'll remember the fight,

   When the Rigid lose all that!

You'll remember the fight,
   When, as rigid Leviathan, you with great enmity: *hated your betters!*
Who took your blows nobly,
   And with kind, wooden, bloody swords, *removed your blind fetters.*

How you'll hate that forgiving blood of Jesus,
   Applied drops at a time on your stony heart!
Until you see it is not the end,
   But the Christ-in-You: Page-Warrior start!

You'll then, *Rigid Ones,* be on the,
   Other side of the sword!
You'll say, as Job did, *I repent!*
   In dust and ashes, Lord!

And if you were particularly mean,
   And hurtful to your dear-brave Warrior-Savior,
God will give you a willow-wimpy sword,
   To fight Leviathan, *inside of your neighbor!*

Oh, woe is me! Oh, woe is me!
   I have but a wooden sword!
From the cross, that victory tree,
   Of Christ, my humble Lord!

You might say,
   Well, it serves me just about right!
Rip me up,
   Leviathan! It's time to fight!

I shall *not* return evil for evil,
   From proud, religiously-rigid man,
He may hurt me, but me *never:* him,
   He'll get what I have in me: I AM!

The great *I AM,*
> Wants to live in us all!
In That Day it's,
> *A strange work: yet not small!*

It's a *BIG* thing,
> When Leviathan pride dies!
And Christ-in-You,
> Trumpets: loud victory cries!

Yet and even much so,
> *Your pride* in all this will be choked: *by your own reins,*
By the smallish sword,
> You'll be given, to do the large work that remains!

Oh, woe is me! Oh, woe is me!
> *I have but a wooden sword!*
From the cross, that victory tree,
> *Of Christ, my humble Lord!*

You might ask me, *where did I learn all this?*
> *That it's a pride-fight and that Leviathan isn't a dinosaur true!*
I learned it by reading the Book of Job,
> From the Warrior-Prophet, not a Page, whose name is Elihu!

This great, but young, Warrior-Prophet,
> Had heard so much talk of churchy-religious pride,
Elihu wrote all of Job's book,
> Yet pride in work: *egoless, he did prodigious hide!*

Elihu hid his authorship,
> *And prophetic voice with Job!*
That following Workmen,
> Would put this in their brain's globe…

Religious-Pride is Leviathan! (It's a smallish issue with beginners!)
    Leviathan is Religious-godly-Pride! (Clericalism makes biggest sinners!)
I write this, as your proud author,
    Oops! That beast is hard to hide!

Where is my bent, old wooden sword?
    God, I lay my heart upon my swag tongue!
Knowledge puffeth me up… in pride,
    Touch me now, oh blood of God's Son!

Oh, woe is me! Oh, woe is me!
    I have but a wooden sword!
From the cross, that victory tree,
    Of Christ, my humble Lord!

But you protest,
    Only Jesus! Jesus alone! He alone *(ALONE!)* is your Savior!
Never you'd let,
    Yourself acknowledge: *He can be greater in your neighbor?*

Can you, then, see now,
    What has been your, and all of milk Churchianity's problem?
Sub-taught leaders vow,
    To never slay their damnable, supercilious, god-pride goblin?

Even tho you say: just reading the bible sans leaven,
    And listening to, or becoming, another Milk-way, Mandarin Madman,
And with Jesus, stuck somehow *(by you?)* in heaven,
    <u>Works to expunge pride</u>? Nope! *It makes naught but bad-bad bad-men.*

So swallow your pride, oh religious daughter or son,
    Prepare to meet your shorter, younger, older, taller… *Much Betters,*
Where dead body is, vultures on you will pick on,
    Your religious pride. *So honor who removes necrotic, hubris fetters.*

You know, only Christ-in-You *(in one)* can do it,
    Almost kill a soul, non-violently, to get rid of religious pride… to move it,
Eyes to see, ears to hear… are a better shoe fit,
    Pride kills. Humility heals. Hear ye, All pride-bots so ill-begot… get to it!

Oh, woe is me! Oh, woe is me!
    I have but a wooden sword!
From the cross, that victory tree,
    Of Christ, my humble Lord!

I'm tired of these dreams. I wake up all groggy. Punch-drunk. What is God saying to me? What does God want me to do? What does God want me to receive? Who am I to fight?

He's going to have to expand my ability to think to take it all in… to drink this overflowing cup.

Sometimes, I feel like giving up my own will and letting Christ-in-You in. *But forget that idea!* That's that little devil Robert Burke speaking to me. And I know my answer to him: *SHUT UP!*

Chapter 10

I didn't ask for this dream…

"Prigipisa, we rocket to an outer-rim planet, land and go to a backwater cantina… or we go to a planet completely built out and find its biggest religious cathedral. What will we find?"

"At the first place: sinners, second: saints?"

"Oh, were it really so! I wish!"

"Saints, then sinners?"

"Neither: Conners. Conners! At both places we will find the normal archetypes of deceived souls conning other deceived souls. It is their preferred game of life."

"There are no sinners or saints?"

"Oh Pringipisa, that is who we all are, only by degrees! Many are mostly sinner, a very small bunch are mostly saint."

"Then what is an alcohol bar for? What is a holy church for?"

"They are to be relatively safe places where lost souls can be… *more found*."

"Found by whom?"

"Found by themselves to be called of God, to choose right over wrong, good over evil."

"And yet we will always have evil… and people who like to do evil?"

"Even as we will always have good… and people who like to do good."

"So then, what is our job? Why have you trained me and been so tough on me to learn languages, the sword, the way of our Creator, the way of politics, religion, the evil elite and base commoners? Why instruct me on churches and bars, like they are the same?"

"Because, dear Princess, bars and churches are life amplifiers. They simply bring out the good... and bad... in people. Take no great joy or offense at what is to be seen and heard... *with eyes to see and ears to hear!*"

"So, I should get married in a trash-planet bar?"

"If you wish! And you are free to meet your future husband in the largest, fanciest cathedral in the galaxy! Ha ha, what a scoundrel he would be... *at first?* The possibilities are *ENDLESS!*"

"Sometimes I think you enjoy running my mind like it's a horse supposed to be Pegasus, only my wings are not there."

"I see them. Your wings. They are strong ones. They'll fly you far, Princess."

"What good is *that*... if my brain isn't fast enough for wings?"

"Thinking about thinking helps thinking. So, tell me: What are un-ascended people thinking about in churches or bars?"

"I am not old enough to go to a bar."

"They are thinking the same. How do we first, stay un-ascended? Secondly, they need something new to believe which will keep them un-ascended while fooling themselves enough to falsely appear as if they, and everyone else in the bar or church, are on the redemption path to glory, honor and heaven!"

"So, you hate them?"

"No, *I love them! God loves them!* They are learning, even as we all learn and grow!"

"So, they muddle through, somehow, amidst all the weeds and wheat... and figure out what is what, good and bad, forgiving the brutality of the winnowing process?"

"*And forgiving themselves. And forgiving God.* Everything. Because humans must learn from the good tree and the evil tree. Both."

"Are we going to meet any ascended souls in bars or churches?

"Most definitely."

"How will we know?"

"By their love toward one another, I think that the Earth Bible puts it. We meet and it seems we are close brothers and sisters."

"Uncle, when I see it... I'll believe it."

"*You'll meet it, and believe it...* if I do my job."

"What is your job with me, Uncle?"

"To give you, to hand you… a recording device with as many high teachings as possible, before I die, *so that In That Day, to steal a phrase,* the highland way of meat continues along with the common way of milk."

"Tio Tio, sometimes I cannot understand a thing you say. Not a thing. Am I supposed to be your recording device?"

"The Earth Bible puts it this way: The blind lead the blind into a ditch. They love to make and hear a lie! Their ears itch for it!"

"So all is doomed?"

"No, all good things are possible!"

"Why?"

"Because we enter now an era, an epoch, a multitude of higher quantum dimensions… where the milk has gone rancid and the steaks on the grill above the coals smell mighty, mighty enticing!"

"STOP! I can't hear another word from you, Tio Tio. My emotions stir my blood. Before I am driven to work the sword on you… hand me one of *The Books Which Are Forbidden*."

"Alright, Little One."

(Tio Tio finds an old book, then a page in the book, and hands it to Pringipisa.)

"Read out loud, dear. Maybe it will take the flush off your cheeks, slow a pounding heart, and soften the flash of some pretty, angry eyes."

I Bought the Broadcasters' Philosopher's Stone

Book #4 of The Books Which Are Forbidden

The Philosopher's Stone, the Philosopher's Stone,
    It will help you preach so exquisite well!
The Philosopher's Stone, the Philosopher's Stone,
    It will help your Christian message sell!

My visitor was a short black man,
    In a worn-out black suit,
Black bowler, black tie, black shirt,
    His voice spoke deep in truth.

You sir, he said, want to be a broadcast preacher,
    Am I not right?
You want donations to fund your airtime costs,
    Who needs a fight?

You need the Philosopher's Stone,
    And all things will turn out well,
In my black bag I've got one here,
    Which you will buy, I will sell.

Now hold on here! Sir, I said,
    You are quite bold and imprudent,
I know a little bit of history,
    Not nothing I learned as student.

The Philosopher's Stone is mythical,
    A story from day's gone past,
A magic elixir potion that makes,
    Victorious solutions fast.

There is no stone as you describe,
    Don't think you can sell one to me,
I don't believe you or that bag,
    Though what's in it, I'd like to see.

The little black man smiled and said,
    You'll see what's in my black bag soon enough,
But first, let's get your eyes open,
    And look at broadcast religion in buff.

The cold, hard, naked truth is that,
    Broadcasting sermons costs many millions,
Not like your church's paltry donations,
    But done right, you might make billions!

Billions? I asked. He said, That's right,
>Billions with a *"B!"*
Just sit on your hands for a minute,
>And listen to me.

Whatever you preach, I don't care,
>You need to sell a certain, crafty solution,
Whatever you preach, say it has power,
>*By viewer's donation,* of a mystic potion!

You'll have to make viewers believe,
>Just a monthly check or credit card withdrawal,
Will fix whatever ills their soul,
>Body, spirit or sap enterprise withal.

Without saying so, you will sell, my friend,
>The witchy-magic Philosopher's Stone,
It is the unspoken thing you sell, they buy,
>That will fund your jet, bank and ritzy home.

Now here's the deal, my time is short,
>So let's get to the quick,
You buy this stone in my bag so viewers,
>Fund its dream of instant fix.

You don't ever give them this stone or copy,
>Or anything like that,
You keep your stone hidden in dark back office,
>To work like magic hat.

I was beginning to get the picture,
>And I grinned like a lusty fool,
So that's how they do it! I laughed,
>>My competition has this tool?

Almost all of them, now you see, my salesman said,
        Have a certified hellacious Philosopher's Stone copy,
As you will in a minute, after signing here in red,
        To sail fast your broadcast in waters un-choppy!

What does the contract say? I asked,
        And what does this dear stone look like?
It says, he said, you sell your soul to Satan,
        And you will be rich as rich is right!

I signed the paper, shirt soaked with sweat,
        I couldn't wait to see this great Philosopher's Stone!
Which has made me richer than I dreamed:
        It is a fist clinched tight, but for middle finger bone.

The skeleton middle finger points straight, defiant,
        Giving the universal sign,
Man deluded thinks he rules o'er slaves compliant,
        Donate to my program fine!

I preach God is certainly sovereign,
        He alone grants whatever He grants!
But that's not how I get donations,
        I say, *YOU* can wear fate's pants!

Donate to my gospel thick,
        My sacred self-dealing message new!
And you will have real quick,
        All your selfish dreams come true!

It doesn't matter what I preach,
        Possessing, as I do, my Broadcasters' Philosopher's Stone,
Bottom line: I sell fearless greed,
        Just donate *to any like me*, and what's mine is in your home!

Dear Lord, why is waking up *SO UGLY?* Why show me the evil works of religion? Why show me a pastor who does not have a clue? Why show me I was entranced with mystic chords of mesmerizing techniques performed on me by people whom I trusted? My blind leaders?

It's so ugly! It's all so dark! Is all… of the Devil? *Was I as blind as my blind leaders? Was I?*

If this is the ascension process, if this is the waking up I need to do, if this is what Robert Burke was talking about in his rotten book and rotten website… then why was I born? *For this junk?*

Was I born just to be excruciated and tortured? How tough do you think I am?

You think I'm a Moses? A Joseph? A Paul? I say I am a man of ease, but you say different?

I say what Eric Burdon and the Animals sang, *"I'm just a soul whose intentions are good. Oh Lord, please don't let me be misunderstood!"*

Chapter 11

I had another nightmare…

"You never win at chess, but I never win at swords. Why, Tio Tio?"

"Because I play chess with you to build your confidence, but with swords I build your respect for things that cut."

"Oh," said Pringipisa to her uncle.

"On Earth a fellow named John Locke said, 'The only defence against the world is a thorough knowledge of it.' There is always a higher game afoot, perhaps played by hidden puppet-masters of great wealth, and that is a game when played against you… you must win. But sometimes, even in a sword fight… it is prudent to lose."

"Win, lose, Tio Tio you speak above the level of my brains. Can you make it relatable?"

"Your mother and father – my brother – died by the sword."

"Did they live by the sword?"

"No, they lived by a very high code. A code they dedicated to you."

"How come I don't know anything about it?"

"Today, Pringipisa, you will."

"Because I'm almost thirteen?"

"Because you're almost ready."

"You say you were born ready."

"Jokes do not count. Are you ready to hear how your parents died?"

"Yes, Tio Tio."

"We were between our galaxy, and Earth's galaxy. We had just visited the Rocky Mountains of Canada, where your mother was born. She was half

Cheyenne, half Irish. As a child our clan had rescued her from human trafficking by Evil Elites of Europe, who wanted her body and blood."

"This is too hard to hear! I am not ready, Uncle."

"Hard truths prevent escape into adult immaturity, Little One."

(Pringipisa slowly nods.)

"My clan raised your mother on this planet and something about Earth makes the finest statesmen and women warriors. She astonished just about everybody with her beauty, her mind and her manifold capabilities."

"Why did she die?"

"Because she had a very strong warrior spirit. Warriors are a different breed among humans. They burn their life's candle at both ends and middle. A warrior's life can be short."

"Why?"

"It is just how warriors are made, along with the heaven-assignments they are given before birth: their soul contracts."

"What's that?"

"It's what a soul is supposed to get done for God while alive, before rejoining in the Great Beyond."

"My mother had a soul contract?"

"A doozy."

"How do you know?"

"She told me about it before she died."

"In space?"

"In space."

"Can we stop? I want to hear this… in ten years. Not now."

(Tio Tio looks at her calmly. There is a pause.)

"Okay, now," said Pringipisa.

"We were halfway between galaxies, and The Great Evil passed close by, on its way to consume another solar system's good. It briefly turned its evil towards our ship… to find the weakest soul on board, my brother – your father."

"No!"

"He succumbed to the evil, turned and cut down your mother – his wife. I turned to cut him down, but he killed himself. And then The Great Evil had passed."

"No!"

"Before your mother died, she told me I must raise you in the way of the Creator. You were to follow your mother in this, and become as she became."

"What?"

"A Master. One of the Creator's Masters. That I must teach you how to die. And lastly, to give you the Precepts of Masters, which she had received from the Creator, and named after you."

"Me?"

"I will tell you this story many times, until it is full."

(Quietly) "Okay."

"Bleeding out, on the floor of my clan's spaceship, this is how your mother died. She said the Warrior's Death Prayer of the Cheyenne Indians of the Rocky Mountains. Her tribe called themselves Human Beings. She said they lived where the snow was white, the grass was green, the wind sang and the sky was blue. *This was her Death Prayer…*"

"Come out and fight!
It is a good day to die!
Thank you for making me
A kind Human Being!
Thank you for helping me
To become a full warrior.
Thank you for my victories…
And for my hard defeats.
Thank you for my vision…
And my ego-cloud's blindness
In which I saw further.
You make all things
And direct them in their ways,
Oh, Grandfather.
Must all Human Beings be in milk,
And never eat steak of the Spirit?
I am going to die now,
Unless death wants to fight.
And I ask you for the last time
To grant me my old power
To make things happen.

Take care of my husband's brother
Take care of my child...
See that they do not go crazy."

"Tio Tio, I cannot stop crying."
"Dry your eyes, Little One. She had a good death. May God grant us such."
"I can't."
"Read then, from The Books Which Are Forbidden. Your mother gave *something*, a gift to its Earth-author."
"What gift?" *(Tio Tio again finds a book from his library, and turns to a page.)*
"They are called *Pringipisa's Principles*."
(Pringipisa takes the book and slowly begins to read...)

Pringipisa's Principles
Book #12 of The Books Which Are Forbidden

1. Every Cause has its Effect; every Effect has its Cause; everything happens according to Law; Chance is but a name for Law NOT recognized; there are many planes of causation, but NOTHING escapes the Law...

2. The Universe is Mental ~~ held in the Mind of THE ALL. While ALL is in THE ALL, it is equally true that THE ALL is in ALL. To him who truly understands this truth hath come great knowledge...

3. Everything flows out and in; everything has its tides; all things rise and fall; the pendulum-swing manifests in everything; the measure of the swing to the right, is the measure of the swing to the left; Rhythm compensates. Nothing Rests; Everything Moves; Everything Vibrates...

4. The half-wise, recognizing the comparative unreality of the Universe, imagine that they may defy its Laws – such are vain and presumptuous fools, and they are broken against the rocks and torn asunder by the elements by reason of their folly...

5. The truly wise, knowing the nature of the Universe, use Law against laws; the higher against the lower; and by the art of alchemy transmute that which is undesirable into that which is worthy, and thus Triumph...

6. Mastery consists not in abnormal dreams, visions and fantastic imaginings or living, but in using the higher forces against the lower – escaping the pains of

the lower planes by vibrating on the higher. Transmutation, not presumptuous denial, IS the weapon of the Master…

7. The wise ones serve on the higher, but rule on the lower. They obey the laws coming from above them, But on their own plane, and those below them, they rule and give orders. And yet, in so doing, they form a part of the Principle, instead of opposing it.

8. The wise man falls in with the Law, and by understanding its movements, he operates it instead of being its blind slave. He who understands this is well on the road to Mastery.

Now I am crying like Pringipisa, but I am more confused. This is the hardest thing I've ever done in my life.

And I don't even know what I am doing. *Something is doing something in me!* And I am not very much in control. No, I am not in control of what is happening. Not at all. And, I am not happy.

Chapter 12

I am an ant. My body has three parts. I think I am a carpenter. Ant.

It is 2,000 years ago. It is Palestine. I am on the sandy part of a trail on a mountain.

Is this a vison, or is this fantasy? Caught up in a landslide. No escape from reality. A Queen rock song runs through my ant brain.

A man comes into view. Many people are following him. He sits on a granite rock next to me. And he begins to speak as a man with authority, not as the mesmerizers and sing-song preachers do in my city. I was astonished at his doctrine. *Was this Jesus?*

As he talked, I crawled – ant-like fashion – to his sandals. I decided to get on his sandals and then onto his robe! And before you know it, I – *an ant (!)* – am up on Jesus' right knee… listening to the sermon on the knee!

"Blessed are the losers who lose their buckets of resentment, for when they let go of resenting the lessons they learn from space and time, they will stop thinking dreams are nightmares and then gain the kingdom of heaven."

(And then Jesus noticed an ant on his knee and he flicked it off with the middle finger of his right hand.)

Ouch, Jesus! We worker ants aren't made to fly! *Don't you know that?* But being as I was flicked only as far as a man can spit, it didn't take me long to find Jesus' sandals again and climb up to his right knee. Again.

"Blessed are they that mourn for becoming and living adult lives as babies or as empty-headed school children, never caring a whit for higher teachings, nor high teachers, nor the excruciating process of becoming masters of the creation which Father God gave men and women to have dominion over… but rather they preach and teach… *anyway the wind blows, doesn't really matter to me. To me.*"

(And Jesus noticed me on his knee again and he flicked me off. It took me a little longer this time to crawl back.)

"Blessed are they that do not despise rebuke and chastisement and flicks of the finger which test your resolve. Do you really want to learn, God wonders?" My mind is playing this song, "*He sees a little silhouette of a man, Scaramouch, Scaramouch, will you do the Fandango?*"

(And Jesus flicked me off his knee.)

Come on, Jesus! Thunderbolts and lightning, very, very frightening me. Galileo, Galileo! Galileo, Galileo! Galileo, Galileo! Galileo, Figaro – magnifico!

As I step through the sands of Palestine to get back on the knee of Jesus, my head is full of the fight between good and evil. The better angels of my soul are having a full-spectrum war with the devil-demons of my same, miserable soul. The war in my head says:

"I'm just a poor boy nobody loves me
He's just a poor boy from a poor family,
Spare him his life from this monstrosity
Easy come, easy go, will you let me go
Bismillah! No, we will not let you go
(Let him go!) Bismillah! We will not let you go
(Let him go!) Bismillah! We will not let you go
(Let me go) Will not let you go
(Let me go) (Never) Never let you go
(Let me go) (Never) let you go (Let me go) Ah
No, no, no, no, no, no, no
Oh mama mia, mama mia, mama mia, let me go
Beelzebub has a devil put aside for me, for me,
For meee!"

I'm back on the knee. I am now comforted. *Resting on the knee of Jesus calms my soul!*

"Blessed are the meek who control their ego during the Isaiah 28 process of winnowing, refining and re-birthing *base souls* into Master-Class servants… humble as the day is long, wise as serpents and harmless as doves … *to the good,* but able to take back vast territories *from evil,* and deliver humankind into greater levels of good being and doing. They shall inherit a beautiful galaxy!"

(And Jesus flicked me off his knee again. *That's it, Jesus!* I see John. I'm going to climb up *John's* knee this time. The war in my head continues.)

"So you think you can stop me and spit in my eye
So you think you can love me and leave me to die
Oh, baby, can't do this to me, baby,
Just gotta get out, just gotta get right outta here!"

"Stay hungry, friends," Jesus said. "Hungry for the Way, even the Higher Way. Use innovative language, examples, parables… the more shocking – *even Bohemian* – the better! It pierces the darkness, the stupor of souls. Don't always stick with the *Blessed are they which do hunger and thirst blah-blah! HA!* Nay rather, use poetry… or something ribald to get the rigid unstuck! Mercy is granted those who are merciful to others."

(And John flicked me off *his* knee.)

Never mind this quest! Damn this quest! I still… *believe and am convinced of…* what I learned as a child: *Who cares. So what. Nothing matters.* Because, when I stop being an ant and I wake up out of this vision, and I am back to being Norman Starmaster, *I will quit everything spiritual!* I may even stop believing in God, which sounds like a good idea to me right now.

But where did John flick me, an ant, off his knee? Wait a minute!!! John flicked me right onto the knee of Peter!

"Blessed are the pure in heart, for they shall see God."

I thought, while on the knee of Peter… Hm… Is that what Robert Burke writes about? *Seeing Christ-in-You.* Is that how Jesus returns… in us? And makes all things possible? And we do bigger works in the Quantum Realms *(I expected no less!)* than the works of Jesus? Right! If we bless a Christ-in-You One, it redounds *(unto and in)* to us. Well, that's a big if. A very Big IF!

(Some man in the crowd burst out loud, "Jesus!" And then another person coughed, then another. Then different women starting shrieking or crying these muffled kind of outbursts. Then it was like a jungle cacophony… with folks yelling "Jesus!" and "Christ!" and coughing and shrieking. Somehow, Jesus didn't mind. Demons were leaving people. *They had to.)*

And I thought: Who wants to be humble enough to see Christ-in-You in another person and bless them for it? Bless *them* for their purity… that lets God inhabit them? *Not ME!* Not nobody. Not any preachers! Not anybody who runs a decent size church… or MEGA CHURCH! Ha Ha!

(Will those coughers and yellers of God's name and loud women *PLEASE SHUT UP?*)

Honor Christ-in-You? Not any preachers I know. They just play Whack-a-Mole Grandees to their captured, entrained and mesmerized audiences! Saying things like, *"Can I get an AMEN?!!* Who would ever be so humble to bless the real Christ-in-You ones? *NOBODY!* That's who. NOBODY, I tell you. NOT ONE seminary teaches that, *or ever will!* Not one preacher. *WHY WOULD THEY?*

(Now the audience is softly whimpering, like they survived a killer storm and nobody got dead. They keep whispering, "Thank, you Jesus!" which annoys me.)

But, then I decided to kind of lock in this *superior* skepticism! *Fahget it!* That's what I thought.

"Nothing really matters, Anyone can see!
Nothing really matters,
Nothing really matters to me
Any way the wind blows…"

The last thing I remember of *this vision* was being crushed by Peter's fingers. He was thorough. *(A Master? But not in a good way? Not yet, anyway?)* He rolled my body between his finger and thumb, and made sure the three parts of my ant body were ripped apart.

What am I learning from all this excruciating? *Beats me!*
I feel very strange. Good and mostly bad.
Some rhapsody.

Chapter 13

"B*elieve in nothing? So you will become."*

I woke up with that thought in my head. Who put it there? *I dunno.*

David said he knew more than the ancients because he kept God's high precepts. Yup, I do study the Bible. And yes, to prove Robert Burke wrong.

So I went for a walk, and again I was watching a play... that weird space play.

A monkey, Tio Tio and Pringipisa are seated at a table. It is afternoon at Tio Tio's mansion.

"Pringipisa, say hello to my friend's circus monkey. The circus came in, and my friend asked me to watch his *'act'* while he does errands in town. The monkey's name is Peter."

"Hello, Peter," said Pringipisa.

(The monkey gave a lips-over-teeth smile.)

"Let's play a game with Peter, shall we? Peter is a very smart monkey, and he knows this game well. The amazing thing is, Peter can count. You'll see! Well, the game is called Peanuts, and I will be the dealer."

"Okay," said Pringipisa.

(The monkey clapped its hands together, still grinning.)

"As dealer, I shall give you each 10 peanuts in the shell. Here, 10 for Peter. And here, 10 for you, Pringipisa. If you need more, I can lend them to you as the dealer."

"How do you play?" asked Pringipisa.

"Princess, put one of the peanuts you have on the table and push it to Peter."

(She does.)

Peter picks up the peanut, inspects it and then takes one of his peanuts, placing *both* peanuts on the table, and pushes the two peanuts to Pringipisa.

"How many peanuts does Peter have, and do you have? asked Tio Tio.

"Nine and eleven," said Pringipisa.

Pringipisa then offers Peter two peanuts. The monkey inspects them, and adds two more from his pile, and pushes four peanuts to Pringipisa.

"How many does he have, and you?" asked Tio Tio.

She counts.

"Seven, thirteen," said Pringipisa.

Then Pringipisa offers three peanuts to Peter. Peter doubles her offer, pushing six back to her in return.

"I count Peter has four peanuts, and I have 16," said Pringipisa.

At this point, the monkey puts a hand, palm up, asking Tio Tio for more peanuts. Tio Tio counts out 12 peanuts and gives them to Peter.

"As dealer, I know Peter is good for the loan. I gave him 12 on loan," said Tio Tio.

"What? Now I count Peter has 16 peanuts…" said Pringipisa.

"Twelve of which are on loan from me, the dealer," said Tio Tio.

"And I have 16. Peter has 16, I have 16," said Pringipisa.

Pringpipsa pushes her entire stash of peanuts to Peter. She pushes out 16, grinning.

"EEE-EEE… AHHHHH-AHHHH!" said Peter, and he pounded the table knowingly.

Peter takes the 16 peanuts Pringipisa offered, adds them to his stash. He then counts out 12 peanuts and returns them to Tio Tio. Holding the remaining peanuts to his chest with one arm, the monkey jumps off his seat, goes to the balcony and begins eating his winnings.

"Peter has 32. I have none," said Pringipisa. "Sometimes I hate you, Uncle."

"I told you, you would," said Tio Tio, smiling.

"Peter returned 12 peanuts to me, so he has 20… all the peanuts you and he started with. Except now he's eating them… This is the game Peter's owner taught him, to use at the circus during the show with someone my friend picks from the audience," said Peter.

"I feel like saying, So what," said Pringipisa.

"Princess, though *God be with us*, we are not *yet* in heaven and there is always hell to pay if we do not watch out for our *own self-interest*, and we do not apprehend or appreciate the *self-interest of others*, or their spouses or their owners. Ask, what are the agendas?"

"I still feel like saying, So what," said Pringipisa.

"Well suppose, dear child, your dream comes true and you meet a perfect man to marry: rich, intelligent, accomplished, handsome!"

"Now, that's the ticket," said Pringipisa.

"Do you get married and hand *your total reins of life...* over to him?"

"What?"

"Or what if in your marriage, he was so enamoured of you, your charm, your beauty, your intelligence...he handed *his total reins of life* over to you? Would you like that?" asked Tio Tio.

"Yes. (pause...) No," said Pringipisa.

"Many people make this mistake with God. *First* they pretend to not believe in God. *Later* they find God and give everything that they can to God, *in order to escape from life and life's responsibilities.* But life finds them and challenges them regardless."

"Who can bear up under your lessons, Tio Tio? Must I think all these things through?"

"Know thyself. And to thine own self be true. And be true to others, even if it hurts you and helps them. Keep your wits about you, and you will do well! Know thine own greed, and you will not lose all your marbles. Know your counterpart's greed and let him keep *what's fair* of his but not *all* of yours. Know who has rigged the game and profits thereby. Because almost always, the game is rigged. In fact, it is surprising when the game is not rigged," said Tio Tio.

"Who rigged the Peanuts game with Peter?" asked Pringipisa.

"My friend who owns him. You see, there is always a higher game afoot. Where is the real profit, in this example, Princess?"

"Uhm, not in the peanuts?"

"Go on..."

"In the tickets sold for the circus? The Peanut game with Peter is entertainment!" said Pringipisa.

"You have captured today's lesson, and mounted it on the wall as a trophy, Princess."

"I suppose there is a poem from The Books Which Are Forbidden you would like to read to me," said Pringipisa.

"I can hide nothing from you now… not that I ever really could," said Tio Tio.

Grabbing a book off his library shelf, Tio Tio finds a page and reads…

A Bigger Game is Afoot! … (In That Day!)
Book #11 of The Books Which Are Forbidden

A bigger game is afoot,
      And I, **_I by God_**, have chased it right down!
A bigger game is afoot,
      And who? **_WHO?_** Who will come around?

Nay! *Nay rather!*
      We think, we know, we pray… you're crazy!
Nay! Nay rather!
      *Stop it! Stop it right now! … We **ARE** lazy!*

A bigger game is afoot,
      And I'm pretty sure… I **_love_** you!
A bigger game is afoot,
      And God has plans… **_above_** you!

_Nay__! Nay rather!_
      We think, we know, we pray… you're crazy!
Nay! Nay rather!
      *Stop it! Stop it right now! … We **ARE** lazy!*

A bigger game is afoot,
      Always, why must you crucify those sent to save you?
A bigger game is afoot,
      It's Christ-in-You, you fear. It **_IS_** what He gave you!

_Nay__! Nay rather!_
      We think, we know, we pray… you're crazy!
Nay! Nay rather!
      *Stop it! Stop it right now! … We **ARE** lazy!*

A bigger game is afoot,
> You ***can't*** get away with the same-old-rotten, vast pudding-pabulum,

A bigger game is afoot,
> The ***proof*** is in the bane-bold rioting, brooding past mayhem-land.

Nay*! Nay rather!*
> *We think, we know, we pray… you're crazy!*

Nay! Nay rather!
> *Stop it! Stop it right now! … We **ARE** lazy!*

A bigger game is afoot,
> God would have you Living Master, so translucent-transcendent-ascendant!

A bigger game is afoot,
> Odd you choose Troglodyte-Morlock, so disaster-unregenerate-unrepentant!

Nay*! Nay rather!*
> *We think, we know, we pray… you're crazy!*

Nay! Nay rather!
> *Stop it! Stop it right now! … We **ARE** lazy!*

A bigger game is afoot,
> You protest you know nothing about… and ***won't*** be told,

A bigger game is afoot,
> Then get yourselves ready, ***fools,*** for a story: so… old-old.

Nay*! Nay rather!*
> *We think, we know, we pray… you're crazy!*

Nay! Nay rather!
> *Stop it! Stop it right now! … We **ARE** lazy!*

A bigger game is afoot,
> My prophet gets so blankety-blank ***tired*** of scribbling theses posts,

A bigger game is afoot,
> **Oh fools, learn of Lincoln at Lyceum!!! says the LORD of hosts.**

(Notes from the Earth author: Abraham Lincoln's 1838 Lyceum speech is most extraordinary, in that 28-year-old Lincoln spoke prophetically throughout his deeply-meaningful, multilayered, utterly profound speech. The deepest part of the speech indicates that mere mortal Americans must ALWAYS be wary of dazzling, self-dealing "Towering Genius" lion family and eagle tribe. Being vastly more intelligent than the Bell Curve norm, such can out-think, out-emotion, out-do us. They will enslave the free or vice versa, it matters not. Ultimately, such evil can implode a Galaxy. The cure? Raising children that are a) generally intelligent (i.e. not gullible), b) moral (Hating all angel-posers!) and c) loving our laws, constitution and God-given liberty's mutual pledge of self-restraint...Oh, Happy In That Day!)

Now I am just walking again... snapping out of that space-play with Pringipisa and Tio Tio.

Hoo Now! A daytime, walking dream!

That's something new to think about!

I may not be as angry at God as I used to be, but I am still just as mad at that Robert Burke.

Burke talks about how the Holy Spirit (he don't call him a ghost) ... teaches all things, and all things includes a mighty, mighty big territory.

Well, Burke never learned nothing from the Holy Ghost, and aren't we supposed to be dumb and happy and not all high-falutin, and not getting changed by all these higher things I been shown?

That's right, I'm still right... and Robert Burke is still wrong.

That's what the Holy Ghost in me says, I say.

Chapter 14

I decided to go to an "America, Wake the Hell Up Tour." It was coming to my city. They had 60 speakers in three days. It included baptisms, patriot tattoo booths, "We're-Still-Angry-With-John-Wilkes" booths, *pay-with-a-credit-card* to get a ticket on "How to Get Out of Debt" sessions... all that and more. I was really looking forward to the all-you-can-eat buffet sessions on dieting, too! That, and buying gold and silver, and junk silver bags and maybe even expensive Challenge Coins with raised images of the speakers, *the VIP speakers.* Wow, was I looking forward to it!

Well, you could name your own price for the general admission ticket. I felt like paying $1,000 so that they treated me better, you know, so I could get selfie pictures with the speakers in the VIP tent. Because there is always a VIP tent, you know? Anyway, that pesky voice in my head said, *"Norman... put your credit card back in your wallet and get your hands off the keyboard."*

Well, before I could put my computer into "sleep" mode... I was having another open vision, dang it.

"Welcome to *Re-Speed Up the American Treadmill Tour,*" said a fat lady with 29 photo ID badges hanging from her neck. I guess she had volunteered lots of these meetings?

She went on, "Here's your driver's license, er... Mr. Stairmaster! What an appropriate name!" Then she attached a lime-green band to my right wrist.

"It's Star-Master," I said.

"Whatever," she said with a fake smile, turning to the next in line.

From the outside, the event building looked like it could hold about 3,000 people. On each side of the entrance were people at temporary tables selling things. *"Patriot Bike Shorts Reduce Chaffing,"* said one sign. *"Choose These Shoes,"* said another. *"Male Sports Bras Stop Bouncing,"* said another. *"Jockstraps and O2 Bottles Here,"* said another. *"Muumuus Make U Confident,"* said another.

"What is going on here?" I asked no one in particular.

"You'll see," said that crazy, voice inside me. (The voice I didn't trust!)

I went in, ignoring the long lines of people buying whatnot from the hawkers at the tables. First thing I noticed, were the video screens. The front, sides and back of the arena had 50-foot tall screens, each maybe 100-feet wide, like a 360-degree theatre. The main stage had what appeared to be an 80-foot-wide treadmill. But get this: there were no chairs for the audience! The entire floor for the audience… was also a massive treadmill!

The screens all had the same image. It was of that of the 1960s black and white, grainy, American Indian in a Feather Headdress Portrait, but interposed with countdown time numbers.

It was ten minutes to showtime! No, nine minutes 58 seconds! No, 56 seconds, No 54 seconds…

"Heh!" a man next to me said, and he knocked my baseball cap off. It fell at my feet. It was my favorite one, because it said *"Speediness is Next to Godliness!"*

"Oh, I guess I wasn't paying attention," I said to the man.

He picked up my cap and said with a laugh, "Don't get entrained too soon, friend! I like to hold out as long as possible, before I get catatonic!" Then he laughed again. It was a pleasant laugh, the kind that made you laugh with him.

"What do you mean?" I asked.

"Once, I lasted eight whole hours… but these events always take ten!" he said.

"Ten what?" I asked.

"Ten whole hours! How long do you think you can last?" he asked.

"You mean stay awake?"

"I mean stay out of a stage-hypnotism, mass-audience-formation trance! That's what I mean," he said.

"I didn't know there was such a thing. What are you talking about?" I asked.

"NLP! You know… *Nuero-Linguistic Programming!* The Nazis invented it after the War… the *Paperclip Nazis* that were invited by the CIA to make the Nazi World Order, I mean our so-called New World Order… their Fourth Reich!

They kinda invented, or perfected Mass Hypnosis Formation… and preachers use it every Sunday, since they latched on to it! *The joke's always on us! Hardy, Har-Har!"* he explained with a laugh.

Oh, this guy is a conspiracy theory freak. I won't pay him no mind, I thought. I said to him, *"Whatever."*

Suddenly, the arena speakers blasted out a huge fanfare of trumpets, at a *hurt-your-ears* volume. Then, "Hell-Hell-Hell-Hell…" said the announcer, real fast, like it was an auction, and the auctioneer didn't want bidders to figure how ridiculous-high the bids was getting… "Hell-Hell-Hell-Hell-Hell-OH! OH-OH-OH-OH-OH-OH-WAH-WAH-WAH-WHA-WAH!" he yelled.

The audience started to come alive. It was stirring them up. Even the oldsters in wheelchairs!

"Hell-Hell-Helloooh-ooh-oh-ooh-ooooh!" said the fast-talking man. He was our Master of Ceremonies, our MC!

"Are you awake?" he boomed the question to the crowd. To me!

"YESSSSSSS," yelled the crowd back to him. *(I yelled it, too!)*

"Welcome to the 50th! Did I say 50th? Yes, I said 50th! TESTING-TESTING… Is this mic working? (He tapped it with his fingers. TAP-TAP-TAP… hurting my ears, the sound system was so loud. Everybody knew he knew the sound system was working. Didn't matter. Nobody called him on it. He was on a roll, just like the audience wanted to have happen? Because it seemed more like he was *working us, the audience, and not really educating us about anything?*) The 50th Ree-Ree-Ree-Ree… Re-Speed Up America's Treadmill TOUR!"

"Yayeeeeeeeee!" yelled the audience in reply.

"You are the 50th State! *The last will be the first!* Are you ready? I said, Are you ready? I SAID, ARE YOU READY? Crowd, say it with me. No, SHOUT IT! ARRRRHHH!" he went on.

(Crowd shouts…) "ARE!"

"YOU-OOOOOOOO!" barked the MC.

(Crowd shouts…) "YOU-OOOOO!"

"READY-EEEEEE!" he barked, like he was a seal, a real seal, training other seals?

(Crowd shouts…) "READY-EEEEEE!"

There was an enormous lever at the back of the stage. The MC walked over to it. Looked like it was six feet long, made of steel, and was tilted to stage left, or to the audience's right.

The MC dramatically came to attention, saluted the US Flag to his stage right (the audience's left) and with a great show of effort, pushed the lever from being *away* from the US flag... and *towards* the US flag (Stage right, or the audience's left) ... where the thing locked into place with a loud *clang-a-ma-bang-bip.*

"BOOM! BOOM-tah-BOOM... BOOM... BOOM!" sounds came through the arena loudspeakers. (Something big and massive was starting up?)

(And shrieks of fear rippled through the audience, back and forth from the stage to the rear entrance-exit, back and forth like fear was alive... and the fear excited the people, almost like they wanted it to come, and they was glad it was here! Like a love of fear, almost?)

"Do not fear, ladies and gentlemen!" said the MC. "Our treadmills have begun!"

And with a lurch and a hitch and a stop and a start... the big treadmills on the stage and under the audience began. Very slowly, at first. We was all walking! Slow at first. *(Faster later!)* The audience was walking towards the stage and the MC was walking toward the audience. *But we would never meet.* Because, we were on treadmills! Everybody was!

My friend to my left was already zombified. He wouldn't respond to me, even if I hit him hard on the back! He didn't last five minutes!

But me, I would last the ten full hours! That's what I said in my head.

There was lots of speakers. There was lots of speeding up the treadmills. Dang, they could go fast! I learned of politics, religion, medical, prepping... and got to see hot, sexy journalist babes, with low-cut blouses and tight skirts talking how they used to report for the Cabal but now are honest as the day is long... and I figure them all to be, pretty easy on the eyes too! But everything kept getting faster, and faster, and faster. The speakers talking faster, walking fast, us in the audience trying to keep up. Folks in wheelchairs doing a pretty good job keeping up with us walking. Then we was running. The speakers were running. Everybody running! Sprinting! Sprinting! GOSH, was this EXCITING! Ambulance people were loading up stretchers of bodies in the back, the ones who could not keep up... I mean on the treadmill, or health-wise. *Whatever!*

Well, I ended up piled in the back, with all the other 3,000 attendees. *Jolly good fun!* And you get to be pretty good friends in that pile of sweaty, overheated bodies piled up. And me? It didn't seem to hurt me none. And get this: *I lasted seven whole hours!*

Next event, I'll last longer.

I can't wait!

Oh, and I was too busy getting improved by speedy talk and walk: *Very Important People,* as to bother anybody to join me against my arch enemy in life... *everybody's arch enemy in life...* that rascal Robert Burke! Thank God, for VIPs... that's what I now say. VIPs are our salvation, they tell me. And... I think I'm a pretty good listener. I learned so much, so fast I can't even explain.

Anyway, like I say, Next event... I'll last longer.

Really, I can't wait!

Chapter 15

*Y*ou don't know it, but as soon as I snapped out of the daytime vision of the *Re-Speed Up the American Treadmill Tour...* I fell into an even worse vision!

I was at another crowded wake up tour, but it was foreign, like Mexican or South of the Border or in Chile somewhere. God have mercy! *These tours had popped up all around the world!*

The MC said "Hola Damas y Caballeros! Me llamo SANCHEZ, *eeeee* hide your wives and your children who are my children! Ha, I am not *keeeeeeding!"*

Somehow, I was understanding whatever the language was... perfectly. How? *I... no se.*

"VAMANOS!" said the MC in a booming, virile voice that only Latin America can produce. I think the women in the audience blushed. The men cowered.

And again I was on the audience treadmill going faster and faster! It was crazy, amigos, loco! *Muy loco!*

"This time I prayed to God, "Jesus help me to run fast enough to get to that lever on the stage and turn the treadmills *DETENIDA! Cerrado! Totalmente fuera ahora.* I mean: *OFF!"*

I kept praying that while I was running, running. And in the vision I was on an audience treadmill in Japan, then in France, or Germany or anywhere around the world where re-awaken leaders were trying to wake up audiences from 3,000 years of Babylonian Cabal control.

Well, in answer to my prayers, the surface of the audience treadmill I was running on *(with everybody)* started to tilt downhill! This tilting was gonna help me run faster! And I would get to the shut off lever, God willing!

Only instead, giant, man-sized SLINKY toys appeared behind everybody running on the treadmill! *Good God!* And these sloppy, big Slinkies *(you know, that children's toy made of loops of spring-wire that can fall down stairs keeping a crazy form?)*... these sloppy, giant Slinkies, they'd fall forward onto themselves, onto their heads. And as they were leaning downhill *(like us runners)* they'd catch up to a runner – and flop down entirely over the runner! Then – POOF! – the runner was gone, the Slinky was empty, and it would flop around to gobble up the next person! *Believe me, the sounds were awful!*

"Not me," I prayed. "It won't get me!"

But then, a Slinky did! It gobbled me up! Inside it, I felt like I was in a science-fiction wormhole... falling, falling, falling.

Then I was just falling through darkness. After about an hour of falling in darkness, I stopped screaming and got a hold of myself. Then I saw a tiny little light below, and I kept falling into it as the light got bigger.

The light showed I was falling into a beautiful, peaceful part of heaven. And then I crashed through a tree, and landed – somehow – onto a really comfortable hammock.

When my head stopped spinning, and I looked around from the hammock *(I was still lying on my back as I had landed)*... I saw next to me was Jesus, in his robes, sitting in an Adirondack chair, smiling.

"Having fun, Norman?" asked Jesus.

"Fun?" I repeated. *(Squirrels were chirping happily about 20 feet away on the grass, but I didn't mention them or nothing.)*

"Having fun on your Quest, Norman?" asked Jesus.

"Is that what you call it?" I said.

"I brought you here to explain a complicated thing, Norman. Just lie back in the hammock, enjoy heaven for a while, and listen to me."

"Okay, Jesus," I said. *(I couldn't really argue, could I?)*

"What your friend said at the first awakening tour was correct. The Nazis who were invited to America after World War Two invented, re-discovered really, a thing called Nuero-Linguistic Programming, or NLP."

(I wanted to fall asleep, but could not.)

Jesus continued: "When a leader has an audience, if they hate me or don't know me or if they were ruined-of-mind by seminaries or universities gone Satanic, they sometimes employ the pernicious techniques of mind control of NLP...

"First, the Satanic-employed leader will say a malaprop saying or joke. They will make an error in fact in the introduction, like saying good morning when it is afternoon. Or they belittle or besmirch the audience, as if they were parasites loathing the host they feed on to live and have their being. Do you know why they call a congregation "Guys" and not "Ladies and Gentlemen," Norman?

"No."

"Because it places the Satanic leader as a Showman, a Showman above the souls of the audience, who now agree to an unwritten NLP contract... the NLP Showman will present an antichrist presentation... as opposed to modelling and enabling a real Christ-in-You operation percolated by our Father in heaven. These leaders will even, on stage, preach and pray with one hand in their pants, in order to dominate the audience. Why, we've even seen them pray at the end of their sermons with BOTH hands in their pants."

"I don't understand, Lord," I said.

"Don't worry, you can revisit this vision as many times as you need to... in order to understand it later. Shall I continue?" asked Jesus.

"Of course, Lord," I said.

"The important thing with establishing Satanic Showmanship, is that the audience doesn't challenge the off-color joke, the rude references or insults to the audience, the shear self-aggrandizement of the know-nothing-but-mesmerization leader. The antichrist leader reaches concord agreement by the audience's quietude, sycophancy and go-along-get-along with any conman-perdition, hellacious thing. None dare mention that their will, the audience's will, is about to be violated without their permission. None dare mention the whole thing is a loathsome witchcraft operation out of the Books and Learnings of the Great Deceiver, Lucifer himself."

"Sounds bad, Jesus," I said, "Whatever it is, you are talking about."

"Next, the son of Satan *(or daughter!)* will cause great hypnotism or mesmerizatoin of the audience... without their permission, always without permission. This fact cannot be over-emphasized. These leaders end up being just magicians, magicians of an evil court."

"How, Jesus? How do bad leaders hypnotize their audiences?"

"By walking left-right. By talking high, then low, then pause and repeat. By building up cascading tension in their voices, then breaking the dam of tension, and then repeating bigger and bigger. Some do it with a f-f-f-f-f-false... stut-stut-

stut-stut – STUTTER! Whoo-heee! *(Jesus paused for a long moment.)* See how it's done?"

"Not at this time, no I don't," I said.

"You will, Norman, you will. The third step can be knocking down a strawman, or a misdirection of any kind. (Can you follow the words I speak, which still are the words my Father tells me to speak?) *POW! Like the 1960s Batman tv show. POW! BAM! BOOM!"*

"What do you mean, Jesus?" I asked.

"Well, the Devil's sons and daughters, posing as so-called 'good' ministers and leaders of God's light… have to proclaim their *bona fides*, their credibility, their good faith, their sincerity, their genuine good intentions, their prestigious abilities. So they pretend they have done great, epic battles and slain giants and dragons. They say they once healed a boy's puppy dog of a tummy ache! They got an old lady to use her turn signals when driving. They say they once returned an overdue library book! They even perchance thought good thoughts about recycling! What heroes they say they are! And the audience MUST support such heroes, right?"

"Doesn't sound right to me, Jesus," I said.

"That is the point, Norm. So the last point of these predictable and Satanic sermon-lessons or leadership pep talks… is to proceed with a *SUGGESTION-ORDER*. The leaders then, having captured the consciousness of low-intellect sheep or people *(whom I instructed leaders, remember Peter my Disciple, to feed-feed-feed, not feed upon like ravenous wolves!)* … the leaders then demand fealty or loyalty to the speaker, or speaker's corrupt organization, by means of pledge to vote, or donation, or pledge to evermore support the shenanigans and mind-control leaders with power, money and anything else they ever ask. And they ask a lot!"

"This sounds horrible, Jesus!" I said.

"Yes, the stench has reached Our Father's nostrils. And He is not happy with it."

"So then, what can be done, Jesus?" I asked.

"Good question, Mr. Star-Master. That is indeed, a very good question!" said Jesus.

(I noticed the squirrels shook their head, and looked at Jesus. Like they understood something I had not yet. Jesus smiled at the squirrels, then at me.)

And just like that... I was in front of my computer screen, about to put it to sleep. Honestly, I don't think any time expired. Not even a second. I put away my credit card. And I tried to remember many other things Jesus told me, but I forgot. Will I remember later? I dunno.

Now, if you think I understand what is happening to me, I don't. I just write what I see, and most of the time I'm not even liking what I see, or what I write.

But I am compelled to write. Maybe if enough pastors or leaders or seminary provosts and such see all that I write, every leader who doesn't want to be fingered as antichrist in practice by Jesus can stop using that "INN-ELL-PEE."

Because Jesus sure doesn't like it. He said God the Father don't like it neither, because it stinks up his nostrils. *I bet I'm not the only one to ever give leaders this kind of message!* These leaders, these pastors, these seminary teachers... they must sure love plugging their ears and giving God the flip of their middle fingers? *Why do they do that?* Speaking of which, my hand that got injured by them chess robots... is all healed and doesn't curl into "the bird" no more.

Weeping. Wailing. Howling. That's what those NLP pastors and seminary leaders ought to be doing. *(Why do I sound like an author I don't like? I don't like that!)*

I'm gonna take a nap now.

Chapter 16

*N*ext morning I decided to give myself a little treat, so I drove over to Carl's Jr., a restaurant chain. Get out of the house, you know. Clear my head.

Well, while I'm enjoying a steak and egg burrito combination meal, a lady customer sitting across from me in the restaurant starts eyeing me with suspicion. Before I can pray her interest in me off, she walked over to my table. She's dressed in English riding clothes, must have just come in from the stables and a morning ride.

"Hello, do you mind if I ask you a question?" she asked.

"Only if you tell me your name. I'm Norman," I said.

"Hi! I'm Carrie with a 'C,'" she said.

" 'C' for Carrie or 'C' for Christ? *(I don't know what made me say that.)*

"That's why I want to ask you a question," she said.

"Go ahead, I'm just eating breakfast," I said.

"Have you recently been with Christ, our Savior?"

"What?"

"Have you been kneeling at the foot of our Lord, on Calgary?" she asked.

"Lady?"

"Did He, our Jesus, give you a word for the church? *Did He?"* she asked.

"What makes you think that?" I asked.

"The glory. *The glory of the Lord is all around you!* And it's fresh! I can tell. It hasn't worn off yet! Quick, tell me the word God gave you for the church!" she said.

"I barely remember a thing, Carrie."

"I knew it!" she shrieked. "I knew it, I knew it! I just *love* how the Lord tells me these things!"

"Hold your horses, horse lady," I said.

"How do you know I love horses? *OF COURSE!* You know because you have been with Jesus! What was it like being at his feet?"

"I dunno. I was lying on my back, in a hammock," I said.

"And Jesus?"

"He was in his robes, comfortable like, sitting in an Adirondack chair," I said.

"Wait! Wait! Wait! I'm calling pastor!" (She flipped out her smart phone and dialled him up.) "Pastor! Pastor! Pastor! It's me… Carrie. Know how Sunday you prayed for a corrective word from Jesus for the church? Uh huh! Well, I'm at Carl's Jr. and I just met a man, Norman, who *has that word for you!* Uh huh! Okay, see ya'." (She ended the call.)

"Carrie?" I said.

"He's coming right over," she said.

"Who?"

"Maximus Paul Doolittle, my Pastor… Pastor of Milk of the Word Shake Church. Know what our motto at church is?"

"No."

"*'We're sweet, 'cause we got it, no sweat!'* Isn't that great?" she said.

"Really?"

"Really! Oh, I can't wait 'til pastor's here! You are still glowing. I see it!" she said.

"See what?"

"You have been on *some journey*. Some journey with the Lord! What is He teaching you? No, wait… don't say anything until pastor comes!" she said.

And so it went as we chit-chatted about nothing until this pastor of hers arrived.

"Thanks for calling, Carrie… I rushed right over," said her pastor, Maximus Paul Dolittle.

"Norman, this is Max Doolittle. He is my pastor," said Carrie.

"Nice to meet you," I said as we shook hands. He sat next to Carrie, across from me at the dining booth.

"Carrie says you have a word from the Lord for the church? When did you get it?" he asked.

"Yesterday," I said.

"Can you tell it to me?" he asked.

"Sure, I guess. *If I remember,"* I said.

"You don't remember?" he asked.

"Well I do, and I don't. A lot has been happening to me," I said.

"Well, err... Norman, try to recall best you can, alright?" he said.

"Okay. I was in a hammock and Jesus was in a chair and he told me about church. Said he would explain a complicated thing to me," I said.

"Good! Good!" he said.

"And Jesus explained what church was doing bad and what it should do good, I think..." I said.

"Yes?"

"He called it, I think, Knee-Linguistic-Programming," I said.

"What?

"He said that's what he wanted church leaders to do, I think," I said.

"And Jesus called it Knee-Linguistic Programming? Write this down, Carrie." (She did, on a notepad the pastor had brought.)

"Yup. NLP for short," I said.

"Okay, got it. NLP for Knee-Linguistic-Programming. Uhm... But Knee doesn't start with an "N," does it Carrie?" said pastor. (Carrie shook her head: No.)

"I dunno. He, Jesus, said Father God was angry to his nose that pastors were not doing NLP," I said.

"Angry to his nose? Jesus said that? Hm... Oh, you mean the stench has reached Father God's nostrils," said pastor with a smile, like he had figured out a great puzzler.

"Isn't that what I said?"

"Yes, Norm. Was there more?"

"Plenty. Jesus, uhm, I think... I think... let me remember... oh, yes! Jesus said first pastors should insult the audience, call them guys, not ladies and gentlemen," I said.

"Well, I say Guys. *Nothing wrong with that!*" said Pastor Max.

"And Jesus said pastors should start off sermons with an off-color joke, and stand with their hands in their pants, pretending it's not rude and not allowed in the US Military and such," I said.

"Well, my jokes aren't *really* off-color. And where else does a man put his hands when on stage in front of people in a church service?" said Doolittle.

"And to use upside down words like incredible, unbelievable... as good adjectives," I said.

"So far, so good... eh, Carrie?" said pastor, beaming a lusty grin.

"Mainly, start with fleshy Showmanship, even test the audience by saying on purpose mistakes like good morning when it's afternoon... or tell them everyone must sit down and be quiet while you remain standing and talk loud, like you – *the speaker* – are special and above the mere, unrespectable souls of the audience. Do anything that breaks logic or the Bible. Do that right at the beginning... *things like that,* Jesus said."

"Well, I never thought of it that way. I just thought... I mean I knew... it works... *Carrie, Jesus was talking inside baseball with this fellow!* Amazing!" said pastor.

"Right, next Jesus said leaders must launch into stage hypnotism... against the unbeknownst audience," I said.

"Stage Hypnotism?" asked pastor.

"Sure. Walk left-right or front to back, or preach in a sing-song voice, or stutter and cause a crescendo of tension, then break the tension like a dam buster, then rinse and repeat! Pretty soon everyone in the congregation will have that frozen, deer-in-the-headlights look!" I said.

"Well, I never heard it described that way, not even in seminary! Are you getting all of this, Carrie?" said pastor. (Carrie nodded yes.)

"Third, Jesus said he wanted every preacher following these methods, to launch into a misdirection or strawman knockdown. Anything that builds up the speaker, no matter how fake!" I said.

"Wow! *What a word from Jesus.* And to think, I was worried!" said pastor.

"Worried about what?" I asked.

"Nothing. Go on," said pastor.

"Lastly, Jesus said every smart preacher who actually believed in God and the prophets..."

"Yes?" interrupted pastor.

"Should end the sermons with a suggestion, more like an order to the zombified, to donate money, or vote for the speaker, or anything ridiculous or unworthy in actuality. *'Simon-says-to-do-and-audience-automatically-does'*... because they have lost conscious control of their best interests!" (Pastor and Carrie looked kind of shocked. I continued...)

"Jesus said His pastors know the best interest of the congregants, so use NLP to extract money and power from the congregants. He called it good clericalism, this NLP," I said.

"Really? Jesus said that?" pastor asked.

"And he said the Russian Commies invented NLP to use politically. But the Russian Orthodox Church rejected it, but the American church leaders and seminary leaders embraced it... embraced NLP as being a good thing. Lastly, sort of like ice cream after a great meal, Jesus said all pastors should end their sermons by praying with BOTH hands in their pants. I remember Jesus mentioning that specifically, I think," I said.

"So, Carrie. *(Pastor paused)* Most services we kind of already do all that..." pastor said.

"I know," said Carrie. (They both sounded somewhat let down, kinda deflated.)

"Wait, pastor! Maybe I got it wrong. Maybe Jesus and Father God and the Holy Spirit were *against* Knee-Linguistic Programming," I said.

"Against it?" Carrie and pastor said together.

"Yah. I think they was against it," I said.

"If they were against it, then this is bad news for the Milk of the Word Shake Church where '*We're sweet, 'cause we got it, no sweat!*' Right Carrie?" asked pastor.

(Carrie was looking intensely at the notes she had made. She shrugged her shoulders.)

"Then we have to change everything! Is this why no one in the church, *myself and staff included,* can understand Christ-in-You?" asked pastor.

"I don't know about that. I get my visions mixed up one day from another. Pastor, if'n what I said makes you feel bad... I'm gonna have to say Jesus was *for* NLP... Yah, that's right! Heaven and the Tricycle God..."

"Triune God, Triune..." interrupted pastor.

"Triune God... wants plenty of NLP, Knee-Linguistic-Programming. I am sure of it!"

"So then, this means nothing will change," said pastor.

"I don't know what you're talking about," I said.

"In other words, all the seminaries and pastors in the US will keep the Prime Directive intact," said pastor.

"What Prime Directive?" I asked.

"That nobody matures: EVER!" said pastor.

"Oh, I get it. I remember, pastor... On tv... there was this show: Star Trek. And Captain Kirk leaves a planet of slaves without photon torpedoing the planet's Cabal Control Center. It's the *Prime Directive.* Do you remember it?" I asked.

"Precisely. *Well you remember, Norman, my boy!* You are right as rain! Ho-ho-ho! I'm feeling jolly as a pirate now! And well we should! *WELL WE SHOULD!* So... friend Norm, it's been great! Thanks for the Word from Jesus! You had me worried there for a moment. *Carrie, shall we?"* said pastor. (And they were gone.)

I went home and threw up my breakfast meal in the toilet. Then I had dry heaves for... *what was it...* about two hours?

No, three.

The whole time I was thinking: In the actual Star Tek tv series, in that show the pastor was talking about... *And Spock on the bridge of the USS Enterprise NCC-1701...* raised his logical eyebrows to indicate the Captain should always obey the Prime Directive to *NOT* help lesser mentalities ... lesser souls... *NOT* help them get up and out of literal or mental slavery... But Kirk actually ordered those photon torpedoes to be fired! "Fire away, Mr. Sulu!"

He really did. *He blew up the computer enslaving that planet's souls!*

I guess James Tiberius Kirk decided, forever, betwixt two things, *and he knowed it...* and he decided. He must have said, "All right then, I'll go to hell."

I wish I could join him. But that's just me being foolish... me being the fool.

I don't know if I'm doing things right. How is a feller to know?

Chapter 17

*T*he next evening… just after sunset… my doorbell rang, so I looked through the vertical windows at my entrance to see who was there. A man about five feet two-inches tall, carrying about 30 pound of fat he didn't need, wearing grey shorts and a grey T-shirt with a stretched out collar. One of his legs was metal below the knee. I wondered how he lost it. His hair was black… medium long.

"Hello," I said after opening the door.

"My name is Aidean," (and I couldn't understand his muffled words that came after that.) "Will you help me?" he asked.

"Say again, what?" I said.

"My name is (muffled sound)… (then) "Will you help me?"

"What do you want?" I asked.

"A ride to the port, uhm, the airport," he said. (While he was talking, I noticed his right eye was bruised. Plus, he had cuts on his arms, and two fingers were bandaged!)

"Have you been in a fight, Mr. Aidean?" I asked.

He looked really embarrassed, nodded and started to cry. But his cry was not sad, but joyful. Very weird. Very strange. He was joyful.

Against my better judgment, I invited him in since he didn't look dangerous, just weird.

"I'm glad you accept me now that you can see me, " he said.

"I'm not sure I accept you, I just let you in because you look beat up to hell," I said.

"That you accept: I am your mighty guardian angel!" he said.

"WH-WH-WHAT?"

"I told you. I am Aidean, the mighty guardian angel of Norman Starmaster!" he said.

"If you are my angel, how come you have a black eye, are cut up, bruised and have a metal leg and need a ride to the airport?" I asked.

"Can I tell you along the way?" he asked.

"I don't know… What proof can I have to know? My momma didn't raise no fool!"

"Well, that's the problem, she kind of did."

"So, tell me a proof I can believe."

"Jesus, Norm… sharpen up, I just did!"

"Momma?"

"Yup, heaven knows… She raised a fool. *But be at peace Norm, she's happy in heaven.*"

"Momma tried…"

"Yes, she did."

"Momma tried to raise me better…"

"Just like the song."

"I don't know about that, nor you! Why do you look like you just lost a big fight, and you're used to it?"

"Because I am."

"An angel? *My angel?* My angel who loses battles?"

"Yes. Yes. Yes. Can we go to the port, the airport now?"

"Nah. I don't believe you're an angel, *nor my angel,* nor that you have, what, heavenly battles you lose?

"Jesus Norm, oh you of little faith! (He casts his eyes upward, listens to instructions I can't hear, wiggles his index finger to the sky left-right, left-right like he's writing notes to himself, nods his head.) He says, *"Okay. Roger that."*

"Who are you talking to?"

"Listen Norm, I'm going to step out in the street. (It was empty, about 8:30 pm. He hobbles, peg-legged, 50 steps away.) And from the street he shouts, "Can you see me?"

"Yes I can see you, Adrien!" I shout from the front porch.

KAH-BOOM-KAH-CLANK – KAH HISS-TAH – BOOM! (Adrian transformed into a Transformer Angel Cyborg. He was about 50 feet tall, had mechanical assisted arms-legs-hands-feet… big cannon-like weapons were attached to his arms and body as well as hung from his back and legs… like a giant star trooper of some kind. He also had big wings with jet-rocket packs… but the wings and jet-rockets were scorched and damaged.

"You... You... You... are an angel? My angel? (Adrian transformed back to being a five-foot two-inch man, a man with a peg leg and right black eye, wearing shorts and T-shirt.)

"You should see your enemies... after I fight 'em," he said.

"What enemies?"

"The ones I fight all the time. Legions of them."

"You fight a legion of enemies for me? *Thousands?*"

"Thousands and thousands at a time, Norm. *I, Adrian the mighty angel of Norman Starmaster – at your service!* Uh, but I still need a ride to the port."

"Wait, if you are an angel, why do you need an airport?"

"Didn't you see my busted jet-rockets and damaged wings... when I was standing in the street... in all battle glory?"

"Yah. I did."

"So give me a ride. Help an angel out."

So I drove him to the airport. But it wasn't where the jets land and people take off. His "port" or portal was on the top of the tallest mountain near my city. He wanted to be dropped off at the trailhead where he could walk to the top of the mountain. He said an *Ezekiel Class Transport* would be there to galaxy-jump any broken angels like him back to heaven for repair and R & R.

"What is R & R?" I asked.

"Rest and Recuperation. *You can thank me later!*"

"Thank you for what?"

"For fighting your legions."

"Legions?"

"Of nasties."

"What are you talking about?"

"Norm, most souls on Earth have a legion, oh about 6,000 give or take, of goods and bads in them. The percentage varies."

"What percentage?"

"Percent good. Percent bad."

"Good or bad what?"

"Oh man, you really aren't with the program yet, are you?"

"What program?"

"Meat. The program above milk. Every soul on Earth... has good adjectives and bad adjectives."

"Adjectives?"

"Yes… attributes. *Remember Jesus?* You met him?"

"If you're my angel, you know I did."

"Right. Inside Jesus there are a minimum – *a minimum mind you* – of 6,000 good attributes. And no bad attributes. None."

"And me?"

"Norm, my job is to fight and conquer the bad attributes in you, *as you do likewise… at the same time, as it were…* when it counts! It's a spiritual fight. When you are called to leave milk land and go toward steak territories of the spirit realm, your soul-spirit-body… gets a cleanup opportunity. And you get assigned a battle angel, a mighty one like me."

"Opportunity for what?"

"For Jesus to indwell you, Norm. But he cannot, or will not, when the majority of your attributes are unclean or even unclean-ish."

"Figures," I said gloomily.

"Well, we're almost at the mountain trail head. I'll hike to the top of the mountain, where I get picked up. It's our portal."

"I didn't know, Aiden. I'm sorry."

"Sorry for what?"

"Sorry I been hanging on to all of my bad attributes."

"Well, everybody seems to like to do that."

"Have I been making your battles worse than they need to be?"

"Not by an arm, but maybe by a leg! Ha ha!"

"You mean that's… my fault?"

"Let's just say I'm paying some dues you don't have to know about when they assigned me… to you. Don't feel too guilty… but run things *more shipshape* and my job gets a lot less ugly."

"I don't know what to say, or feel."

"Here's one of the best and worst things about your attribute of being one stubborn cuss. You being so dang stubborn all the time. Reverse it."

"Explain."

"When you are wrong, lose the stubbornness. When you are right, hold on to it loosely, *so as to be flexible with your stubbornness.* Right now, you're doing mostly the reverse. Fix that, and my battles get way easier."

"Okay, I'll try."

"There is no try, only do… (He said it in a Yoda voice) And one more thing."

"What."

"Robert Winkler Burke isn't the enemy of your soul. *Stop now, don't argue with your angel!* (I was gonna.) Here is a secret I would like to tell you about Robert Burke. (But I shut up when my angel was telling me a secret on my arch enemy.) My job with you is a lot easier job than Burke's angel had… *fighting his damn demons!* It was epically worse! Heaven was shocked! No, compared to Burke's angel, my job with you is much, much easier. *You know more than you know, Mr. Starmaster.* Bye!"

"Goodbye."

I drove off.

And I said to no one in particular, "I do? I know more than I know?"

Things were getting curiouser and curiouser.

Chapter 18

I was standing in front of three pastors. They were in my home. It was afternoon. They were sitting at my dining room table, but about to leave. We had been talking for some time.

"Pastor Bill, here is an envelope with $2,000 in it. Buy 100 copies of Robert Burke's book, give it to your congregants and report back to me their findings," I said. (Then I turned to another man.)

"Pastor George, here is an envelope with $3,000 in it. You can buy 150 copies of Burke's book. Do the same. Get reviews," I said. (Then I turned to the last man.)

"Pastor Sy, here is an envelope with $5,000. Buy 250 books and do likewise," I said. (Then I addressed all of them.)

"Now… I expect to hear back from you with 500 reports… 500 honest reviews, that's all I ask. Give me 500 reports on the ideas of Robert Burke. Good day gentlemen. Go with God," I said.

After they left, I sat down at my dining table. Then I screamed as loud as I could! I screamed to myself…

"YOU IDIOT, NORMAN! IDIOT! Idiot-Idiot-Idiot-Idiot! WHAT DID YOU DO WITH THAT MONEY? AHH-H-H-H-H-H-H-H-H-H!"

[EARLIER THAT DAY…]

(Sy, at my front door.) "Hello Mr. Norman Starmaster. We are pastors. I am Sy, this is George and… Bill," said the man.

"Hello, why have you come to my home?"

"To give you gifts," said Sy. Then turning aside, he said, "Bill?"

(Bill handed me an envelope. It had $2,000 in cash!)

"George?" says Sy.

(George handed me an envelope. It had $3,000 in cash!)

"Why are you giving me cash?" I ask.

(Sy handed me an envelope. It had $5,000!)

"Why are you giving me ten grand?" I ask.

"Because we talked to Max Doolittle. He said you were a prophet," said Sy.

"I am not a prophet."

"*Everyone who is in the Light is essentially a prophet...* That's from the Russian Poet-Warrior Lev Ivanov!" said Sy.

"What makes you think I'm in the light?"

"First, you hate Robert Burke, whom we also hate. *Every pastor we know who knows him... does.* Second, you confirmed that the style and way of Pastor Max at the Milk of the Shake Church was perfect, pleasing God and something we should all copy. We believe you have been on visits with Jesus and we see His light in you also. We give God all the glory!" said Sy.

"Wait. Wait a minute. Come in, let's sit at my table," I said. (They did.)

"How do you start your services, pastors?" I asked. (George and Bill looked at Sy, telling him to speak for them.)

"Typically, we begin by insulting all the women present. We'll say, '*Guys*, I have a *cool* sermon for you!'" said Sy.

"STOP. Never say *Guys* when addressing women and men in a church," I said.

"Why?" asked Sy.

"God made man and woman, men and women. He did not call them *Guys,*" I said.

"Okay. What should we call them?" asked Sy.

"Beloved men and beloved women. Or ladies and gentlemen of God. Or beloved of God. Anything indicating respect and avoiding disdain or insulting with familiarity," I said.

"This will not be easy for us, but we can try," said Sy.

"What do you do after addressing the audience?" I asked.

"We tell a joke, something off-color."

"STOP. Never do that again."

"Next, we have a habit of throwing out a brain-stopper... like saying, 'Turn to your neighbor and say *I'm trying hard not to hate you.*' Things like that. We know we have succeeded if we hear uncomfortable laughter. Then we know we are spot on!" said Sy.

"STOP. Never do that again."

"Okay. So then we launch into our scripture message. We like to order the audio-visual team in the back of the church to... *Throw up John 3:16 on the screen*... you know, to be edgy... edgy and current with the culture!" said Sy.

"STOP. Never be edgy like that again."

"Then, when delivering our so-called message we walk left-right, or front-back, or talk in singsong, or like we are professors talking baby-talk to infants, or we stutter and build up tension only to release it again and again. Want to learn how? We could teach you!" said Sy.

"STOP. Never do that again. It is stage hypnotism."

"Okay. *Wow. We didn't expect this!* Next we do a misdirection... something involving a strawman knockdown story where we glorify ourselves and our operations, however devoid of true meaning that would help or feed our sheep. We enjoy abrogating our jobs as shepherds... we'd rather be entertainers! We learned all this in seminary," said Sy.

"STOP. Never do that again."

"Then we always close with a demand or a suggestion-demand for money... money for more nugatory buildings, money for missionaries to go where they've gone for 300 years pretending nobody had been there before them, we spend money on things that never change... money, money, money for anything and everything... money! Oh, then we pray, usually with both hands in pants. I forgot to say most of the time on stage, we have one hand in and out of our pants pocket," said Sy.

"STOP. Never do those things again."

"When what do we do?" asked Sy.

(That's when I gave the pastors the money to buy Burke's book. The pastors seemed glad to get their money back, but they didn't seem happy with anything I said when I was full of the Light. Oh well. I really don't understand anything that happens or anything I say or do when full of the Light. I didn't realize people noticed any of *that Light* in me. Maybe I should start wearing a hoodie, and hide my face from people. Because people bother me.)

So I ate some dinner, and after that I decided to talk to myself. That always helps.

I thought: God, I hate myself. What am I doing? Who is in control of me? Who is *in* me?

Isn't Burke wrong about Christ-in-You? Those 500 people who'll read his book, they'll tell me! I know… they'll tell me Burke is wrong. So very, very, very wrong.

Why is Burke wrong? Because there is no mind-meld with God! There is no Mind of Christ to be at one with. Maybe in heaven, but not nobody on Earth can do it. Not me. Not you, who is reading this. Not nobody. Everybody agrees. And when everybody agrees with something, that proves it is true! Everybody knows that.

There is no *Mind of Christ* to be at one with, not while we are on Earth! There is just nothing. Sure, there is God in heaven… but leave God in heaven be. He ain't indwelling us! He is just judging us, if we are to go to heaven or to hell. That's it. That's all. That's everything.

There is just nothing at all, because I say so. And the power of my say so is great, because I say so. If I say something is nothing, then it is nothing. It ain't something, it is nothing. Nothing.

Wow! I feel great! Empowered! Impactful! Relevant! Leaning into Truth! Unpackaging God! If I had a screen, I'd order up the A-V people to throw up a scripture on it!… I'm in the pocket, now! God's in my pocket, and I know that pocket! It is what I say it is! Believe me, brothers! Believe me, sisters! GLORY! GLORY BE TO GOD! Worship me, I mean Him!

Good! Now I'm getting back to my old self! *This*… is how it is supposed to be!

And I'll conquer Robert Burke yet, by God! And by God, I will!

Oh, Happy Day!

Think Like an Advanced Christian?

Pooh on that idea! To hell with it, I say.

Chapter 19

You don't know this but it was only eight days later them same three pastors come knocking on my door, midafternoon.

––––––––

"Hello," I said when I opened the door to them.
"Hello!" they beamed back at me. They looked real pleased with themselves, like they knew something I didn't.
"I ain't taking no envelopes of money from you," I said.
"Oh no, Norman Starmaster, we have something much better than that," said Sy.
"Okay. Come in. Sit down. What are you here for this time? Don't expect nothing from me," I said after we were all seated at my dining table.
"We have happy reports for you, Norman," said Sy.
"Like what?" I asked.
"From your preaching advice," said Sy.
"Well, I am sorry about that. Which version did I give you? I get them mixed up," I said.
"You mean you don't control, or know, or remember what you're saying?" said Sy.
"Something like that. Sometimes I'm *me-myself* talking. Sometimes Jesus gets in a word or two. Sometimes the opposite. Sometimes it is I AM, like the Great I AM. Fellers, I'm going through some hard changes right now," I said.
"Well, at any rate… you made our congregants happy. Very happy," said Sy.
"I did?"

"*Splendiferously*. Not only did all our congregants cheer at losing the bad preaching styles we adopted, but special businessmen in our audience took note," said Sy.

"Took note? What kind of note?" I asked.

"Monday after Sunday, just a day later... each of us got a call to meet at the Steak Bistro Tre-Plus Restaurant to huddle up... we three pastors with the three biggest donors in our separate churches! Of course, our donors talk to each other. They were delighted about the good things that happened in our new sermons! So they wanted us to meet. Occasionally we meet like that at their request. And we listen to them," said Sy.

"What did they say?" I asked.

"They said they were very much moved by our dropping NLP memes, ways and tropes of brain control. We didn't even know what NLP was, or that we were using it. We had all just learned it in seminary, and knew it worked to get donations and involuntary cooperation from the sheep!" said Sy.

"It's Neuro-Linguistic Programming done to unwitting audiences. Jesus told me that," I said.

"Right. That's what they told us, the businessmen. So then they said *let there be a financial reward for the correction of church!* They said that," said Sy.

"What did you say?" I asked.

"Well, as you businessmen know... each of our churches is renting, but to buy them would be close to $2.5 million. We asked the businessmen to pay that for us, for only just $7.5 million," said Sy.

"And so they did?" I asked.

"No. Instead they asked... What about Norm Starmaster? Does *he* have a mortgage on his home? We said what you ask is impossible. It is impossible to find out, or pay off, or do anything about. That's what we said," said Sy.

"What did the businessmen say?" I asked.

"Well, they looked disgusted with us and one man called his executive secretary. In about 60 seconds, the executive secretary called him back. So the businessman said Norman Starmaster owes $250,000 on his home mortgage," said Sy.

"Well, they are right. I do," I said.

"No, you are wrong, Mr. Starmaster. The three businessmen paid off your mortgage by way of saying thanks to you," said Sy.

"They did? Did they pay off your church mortgages?" I asked.

"No. They said first things first... *Honor unto whom honor is due.* We asked where they learned that. They said *business mentors* taught them to *honor whom honor is due...* and also Romans 13:7. We said we tried to give you $10,000 but you returned it," said Sy.

"Mind if I call Wells Fargo?" I asked.

"Go ahead," said Sy, smiling. The other pastors grinned at each other.

Sure enough, my home mortgage was paid off. Also the loan on my SUV. Also my credit card balance. I was debt free!

When I hung up the phone, I was speechless. What could I say to them? What was happening to me? When I came back to myself, I figured what to say.

"Did you buy them books of Robert Burke for your congregants?" I asked.

"Yes sir, all 500 and more. They will be passed out this week. What else should we do?" Sy asked.

"Uhm. Uhm. Uh. Darn it, thank the businessmen for me. Tell 'em thanks. Tell 'em thank you very much, except I don't know what for they did that. Tell 'em they make me angry. No don't tell 'em I'm angry. Just tell 'em thanks and leave it at that," I said.

"Will do, Mr. Starmaster. We thank you and we will thank the businessmen for you," said Sy.

"NOW, GET OUT OF HERE!" I yelled. (I was getting angry. Didn't have no control.) "Good is not supposed to happen to me or you by following the advice of Robert Burke! I told you I got my messages mixed up*!" I said.* "I got it right with Max and wrong with you three! *Just get out of here!"* I yelled.

"But everyone at church was so happy not be stage-hypnotized! The women appreciated not being called *Guys* or have to listen to off-color jokes," said Sy.

"People were healed!" the other two pastors said at once.

"Healed? Did you say healed?" I asked.

"Sure. We were surprised, too!" said the other two: George and Bill.

"Look Norm. For all three of us, when we stood at the back of our churches after preaching... and we met people, they asked us who changed us and we told them..."

"NORMAN STARMASTER!" all three said together.

"And that's why we are inviting you to speak at our three churches. The people want to meet you... *and be healed!"* said Sy.

"I don't heal nobody," I said.

"Oh no, Norman. That's not true! Why, after the hour we spent with you last week, I stopped needing glasses," said Sy.

"I lost a heart problem needing surgery, that's what my doctor told me yesterday," said Bill excitedly.

"I was due for hip replacement, but not any more… my doctor told me two days ago I'm good!" said George.

"That's it. Get out of here. Are you quacks? Charlatans? Faith Healers? You expect me to believe that?" I asked.

When they were leaving, they kept saying… "It's true! It's true! The Christ-in-You healed us! The Christ-in-You healed us all! The Christ-in-You can heal our city, our state!"

Why do good things keep happening to me? Dang it. *When will it ever stop!*

This is not turning out like I expected it to turn out. No it is not.

But all is not lost! It's pretty easy to destroy people, or I mean… destroy the reputation of people. There's more ways than one to skin a cat! I don't know at this point, if I'm gonna prove Robert Burke wrong or Christ-in-You wrong. *Either way works for me.*

But I *do hope* people stop getting healed. That's embarrassing.

Life is percolating now, but not how I want it to. Life is percolating like God is in it, and I'm in it… some angelic part of me in it.

But I'm NOT happy. I want more control. *All the control…* like how it used to be. Just me.

This having *good in me,* using *good in me* with a *Greater Good visiting inside me* to do things, well… I don't know about that.

But I'm going to find out.

Chapter 20

*I*n this dream Pringipisa was an older teenager, but still learning from Tio Tio at his estate in some other solar system or the other. *Didn't he say we are in a different Galaxy? Hm…*

"Pringipisa, you have learned the three things on Earth that made one country the greatest? And… who told of these three things?

"A man named Abraham Lincoln," said Prinipisa.

"And what three things did he say a nation needed to be great?" asked Tio Tio.

"Children had to be raised to be generally intelligent, moral and lovers of laws and the US Constitution," said Pringipisa.

"Very good. But was that enough to conquer Satanic people with infinite wealth and power obtained from Babylonian banking schemes?"

"No. The US fell victim to those infinite wealth, infinite power families of Babylonian wealth systems," said Pringipisa.

"Even though… even though the US people in Lincoln's time were somewhat generally intelligent, moral and lovers of laws and the US Constitution?" asked Tio Tio.

"Yes. Even though the people had all that in the 1860s, by the beginning of the 21st Century AD, the US were a people fully and completely enslaved by mental brainwashing."

"Mentally enslaved?" asked Tio Tio.

"Mentally enslaved, Uncle."

"So, have I taught you… what did they lack? What did the people from 1865 to 2,000 AD in the US need, which they lacked?"

"Well, Lincoln said to beware *Towering Genius* which mentally enslaves all. They needed to be aware that Towering Genius could *con* people, making certain families infinitely rich, which made them infinitely powerful."

"Indeed. How did those families obtain virtual, infinite wealth and power?"

"By creating globally-networked Central Bank systems whereby these certain families printed currency out of nothing… while making it illegal for governments to do so… then loaning this printed-out-of-nothing money to governments… they charged interest and fees to do so… and these loans with charges had to be paid by citizens, common citizens."

"What happened when the government… using taxes paid by citizens… paid back the principal of the loans… plus interest and fees?"

"These certain families kept the interest and fees, but destroyed the principal loan amounts paid back to them,"

"And how do we know this, that they destroyed the principal amounts repaid?"

"People outside these systems don't know for sure, because the Central Bank families usually never showed their books to governments, nor anyone but themselves."

"So they acted above governments' laws and morals? *They acted as gods?* Tell, me, Pringipisa, what always happens to sentient beings who have infinite money and power to act as gods?"

"They always become Satanic, fully so."

"And what does it mean to become fully Satanic?"

"It means usually they have ceremonies to have sex with and kill children, and it means they dedicate their infinite money and power to depopulate and destroy life on their worlds. This is the inevitable result of Babylonian Banking systems: all destroyed."

"So, it is a sad, but typical result?"

"Yes, so sad, Tio Tio!"

"But if people on a planet are lucky, they can throw off such an evil system?"

"Yes, God willing," said Pringipisa.

"Yes, that is the answer: if God is willing. But isn't God always willing to do good?" asked Tio Tio.

"Yes, but the people must be mature, ready and desirous," said Pringipisa.

"Desirous of what?"

"To see the Truth."

"Is Truth hard to see?"

"Tio Tio, that is one of the main lessons you have given me," said Pringipisa.

"What factors enable a planet to get rid of infinite wealth and power, these Satanic Systems of Brainwashing Control?"

"Well, good leaders do it, good leaders who go beyond mere general intelligence, morals and love of laws and constitutional protections," said Pringipisa.

"Go on," said Tio Tio.

"Well, you've told me it is three things. A martial and high strategy discipline for the body teaching kindness, healing and restoration to enemies which one fights in a state of strength and honorable-right courage... a knowledge of brainiac cons which normally enslave souls combined with superior governmental concepts where no man is the judge in his own case, and lastly... the steak of God indwelling... not milk memes and ways of religion *followers of God*... but nay rather... what on Earth is called the *indwelling of Christ-in-You*, where God indwells more purified souls which are then congruent at determined levels with good and conflicted at determined levels with bad, as per two-way communication made possible with the Creator of All," said Pringipisa.

"Can these rather large arenas with rather large subjects be abbreviated, for the sake of getting a handle on vast concepts, and how to win epic wars between good and evil?" asked Tio Tio.

"Well, that author on Earth, Robert Burke, has abbreviated Lincoln's Lyceum Speech recommendations where children are to be raised general intelligent, moral and lovers of laws and the US Constitution. He abbreviates it: GIMLLC."

"Would GIMLLC then be milk in political understanding?" asked Tio Tio.

"I guess so, yes."

"What is the abbreviation above that... in the steak territory of understanding?"

""Well again, this Burke on Earth calls it S76C. It's S76C above GIMLLC."

"What does S76C stand for?" asked Tio Tio.

"S is for Systema, Russian Martial Art Systema (but this represents any great martial understanding, like The Art of War of Sun Tzu or of General Lucius Quinctius Cincinnatus who twice gave up being an Emperor, even as George Washington did give up twice the opportunity to be lifelong king). Then, 76 is for the triune doctrinal papers of 1776, 1787 and 1791. C is for Christ-in-You. *S76C.*" said Pringipisa.

"On Earth, what are the 1776-1787-1791 documents of doctrine?" asked Tio Tio.

"Well, 1776: the Declaration of Independence. 1787 was the US Constitution. And 1791 was the US Bill of Rights," said Pringipisa.

"And where does the abbreviation C-I-Y, Christ-in-You, come from?"

"It comes from the Earth Bible, Colossians 1:26-27, but similar terms are found in *steak-not-milk* texts in many other places," said Pringipisa.

"This Burke was a religious thinker?" asked Tio Tio.

"Yes, his work began with explaining how to go from milk to meat, and he called his work In *That Day Teachings.* He abbreviated it ITDTs."

"So, ITDTs explain that Lincoln's milk of GIMLLC was defeated by Towering Genius of Babylonian Banker cons?"

"Yes, Burke said the defeat of good government began immediately after the Civil War which Lincoln overtly won... but the whole thing – *that war* – might have been a ruse to install mental slavery in modern times... instead of the ball-and-chain slavery of ancient times. In other words, Lincoln was used by greater and more evil powers to win the elemental fight against chattel slavery... in order that the greater and more evil powers could install mental slavery, which is a far worse and more complete slavery system," said Pringipisa.

"So was this 3,000-year-old slavery system of control... first ball-and-chain and then total mental slavery... was this 3,000-year-old slavery system going to be defeated?" asked Tio Tio.

"Well, Burke said, *Yes it would.* He said the evil of Towering Genius Babylonian slavery would be defeated by S76C people. They would be an advanced group of doers who were more than a match against the downloaded plans of Satan of the Babylonian Mental Enslavement Control Cabal," said Pringipisa.

"Yes. Correct. Burke said God could raise up a *GOOD Towering Genius* team of accomplished souls who, in the steak of things, outwit and handily, humanely, and efficiently defeat the bad guy control of *his planet,* Earth," said Tio Tio.

"Did that happen?" asked Pringipisa. "Did their White Hat Alliance successfully use sixth and seventh generation warfare techniques?"

"Yes, it happened just as Burke wrote about," said Tio Tio.

"So, everyone on Earth must have really loved the team of good people who did that!" said Pringipisa.

"No, actually Princess, many people of religion hated and despised the good teams of intelligent, high-strategy people of outstanding *Love Vibrations*... the amazing White Hat Teams," said Tio Tio.

"Why? Why did Christians and religious people hate the White Hat Teams?" asked Pringipisa.

"Because milk religion, especially milk Christianity, had seminaries and preachers who really didn't respect each human soul, and because they didn't... they didn't believe government was supposed to guarantee the rights God gave each human soul, so they despised the White Hat Teams who returned good to Earth in large measure," said Tio Tio.

"I don't understand," said Pringipisa.

"An Earth proverb is... *Divine Providence only works through human instrumentality.*"

And people in milk religion hate humans who accomplish great good?" asked Pringipisa.

"At first, yes. In truth many milk people have very little regard for any humans, they only love God," said Tio Tio.

"Well, it is a start," said Pringipisa.

"Yes, it's a start," said Tio Tio. And they both smiled.

I wish I did not sleep. Then I would not dream.

I never dreamed I could understand this kind of talk. *But I fear I now do!* Oh well. How come my brain never tolerated, much less understood... this elevated kind of discussion? *How come?*

There is an old African saying, *"When an old man dies, a library burns to the ground."* Well, in these dreams I wish that on Tio Tio. Who does he think he is, dominating that young woman?

So, I think I'll just go to churches which only preach salvation. And I'll ask the pastors of *Only Salvation* churches to pray: *I never go to sleep or dream again.* That will fix things, won't it?

If only Pastor Far Reach at *Life is Life, Really-Really Church* believed I was saved, and he would pray the way I want him to, and not just always pray for everybody and everything to be saved.

Oh well. One can hope.

Chapter 21

I called the Televangelist Dream Network phone line for prayer. First they asked for money. Then I asked for prayer: *to stop my dreams!* Next, I fell asleep and I was watching that boring space play in another dream… *dang it!*

"Tio Tio, why did the Central Bank families end up worshipping Satan and striving to depopulate their planet?"

"Because of one of Earth's wisdom sayings: *Power corrupts and absolute power corrupts absolutely,* said one of their historians, Lord Action," said Tio Tio.

"Why was it so hard for the people of Earth to shake off evil mind control of these infinite wealth and power families?" asked Pringipisa.

"Because the families did not hurt Earth's population in any *one particular way or method,* lest it be discovered, and the people fight back successfully. Instead, it was a delivery system of death by a thousand cuts. People were culled by fraud medicine, fraud climate laws limiting production of goods, fraud voting, fraud media, fraud food… everything fraud!"

"How could they do that?"

"Easily, with their infinite money which they printed and controlled," said Tio Tio.

"Well, the details of all this makes my head spin a few times, and then want to turn off," said Pringipisa.

"Yes, my child, great and hard truths are quite difficult to absorb and fathom at first! But let us now talk of Spirit," said Tio Tio.

"Spirit?"

"Yes. The Earth Cabal's plans and operations of *depopulation-by-a-thousand-cuts*... de-spirited humans. They feared each new deleterious thing! Their lives and world went from any good thing is possible and ameliorating... to all is getting worse and life-robbing."

"So what was the answer to that?"

"Maturity. Maturity is the answer to all life's problems... *maturity in God!*"

"So, did people mature?"

"The exigencies of overturning 3,000 years of Babylonian mind control caused a bifurcation of souls on Earth."

"You mean people's souls split in two?"

"No, Princess... A third of the people refused to see higher truths because in their entirety of life-being on Earth, they had pledged allegiance to unending immaturity of their own souls."

"*Oh no!* What happened to them?"

"Short answer: They walked willingly into the Cabal's *death-by-a-thousand-cuts* depopulation operations. Most of this third group... over time, did not survive. And when they perished, they remained steadfastly and doggedly immature of soul."

"What of the other two-thirds of humanity?"

"Pringipisa, the top third faired very well indeed! They enjoyed the *excruciatingly vigorous chrysalis trip from milk to meat,* from three-dimensional life to great dimensions beyond... they ascended, pineal gland and all, thank God!"

"And what of the middle one-third group?"

"They muddled through, somehow. They tried to half-stay in the milk, and half-go into meat territories. As the Earth Bible puts it: *A double-minded man is unstable in all his ways.*"

"Did church help the people on Earth during this time?" asked Pringipisa.

"At first, not much. Burke's writings explained that by the beginning of the 21st Century, virtually all seminaries and church leaders had dedicated themselves to gross immaturity in God for as long as possible," said Tio Tio.

"What happened?"

"Well, the people, *as civilians,* rejected immaturity and remedied the corruption of state. Much later, seminaries and church leaders reluctantly admitted their stubborn lust for permanent immaturity... and they finally matured into meat territories of Spirit, *at least some portion of them did.*"

"Well, better late than never!" said Pringipisa.

"To which I always reply… Earlier is easier, and late makes everything harder… *but to each his own.* God loves everyone, and God made a universe designed to mature all life!"

"Tio Tio, not another word, please. No more lessons for today. My brain can't handle any more information, and I'm starving," said Pringipisa.

"Yes, lessons are over for today. Many times ago, I brought some special seeds from Earth. Would you like to tase something sweet?"

"I would. What is it called?" asked Pringipisa.

"Watermelon!"

Sweet and easy, I like. Hard and unfathomable, I don't.

It bothers me I am *beginning…* to understand these dreams more fully. *Before,* my brain never could! I thought nobody could ever understand such highfalutin notions. I was positive nobody could understand anything like what higher-up bad guys do with their rotten plans from hell. *Before,* my brain was at full capacity. I could watch tv, *but not think through a Tio Tio lesson!*

All of this is *such a bother.* A bother. A bother. A bother. What a great bother!

Sometimes I just want to eat a bowl full of cereal and milk, *but without the cereal!* Yup! Just cool, clean, wholesome milk. Lots and lots of sweet, old, lovey-dovey milk! That is spelled M-I-L-K! *MILK! YES, MILK! I LOVE IT, LOVE IT, LOVE IT!* **I LOVE IT!** *I truly do!*

But no. It's dinnertime. And my stomach *(or my gut?)* doesn't want milk, even though my mind does! Who's in charge, here anyways? I say: my mind, that's what I say.

So, why am I driving to my local steakhouse, *where they are getting to know me?* Huh?

Chapter 22

You don't know it, but those three pastors won't leave me alone. Knock-knock. Who's there?

"Oh, it's you again."
"Hi Norm," the three pastors said.
"Come in, sit down. What is it this time?" I asked.
"It sure is good to see you. It's been 90 days!" said Pastor Sy.
"That long."
"Yes sir, three months. And boy, are we happy!" said Sy.
"Glad somebody is," I said in my most gloomy.
"Well, revival keeps breaking out!"
"What?"
"We found out a *fascinating* discovery! *As long as we break the rules...* taught us by seminary professors, revival keeps breaking out at our churches!"
"Sy, I have no idea what you are talking about."
"Remember the 500 books you had us buy?" asked Sy.
"100 for my church!" said Pastor Bill.
"150 for mine!" said Pastor George.
"Oh," I said, just barely remembering.
"And 250 for mine!" Said Sy.
"Oh well, did they hate it, like I do?" I asked.
"Don't kid with us, Mr. Starmaster, our congregants *loved* the book, like we told you last time," said Sy.
"Gentlemen, I can't tell you how that makes me feel," I said using my *not-happy* voice.

"Well, that book... that book of Robert Winkler Burke, it says to *NOT* preach the texts of the Bible with a spirit of *FEAR!*" said Bill.

"And to *NOT* preach the texts of the Bible with a spirit of *GREED!*" said George.

Then Bill and George said together, "And it says to *NOT* preach the Bible texts with a spirit of..."

"*LAZINESS!*" said Sy.

Then all three said together, "That's what our seminaries taught us to do! *To get money!*"

"I filled my congregants with fear using texts of the Bible, you know, adding end-times ink-blot-imaginings. Just a bunch of... FEAR! But the book you recommended said to *STOP THAT!*" said Bill.

"And I... I filled my congregants with greed using texts of the Bible, you know, adding give-to-get-whacky prosperity preaching. Just a bunch of... GREED! But the book you recommended said to *STOP THAT!*" said George.

"Me? I filled *my congregants* with laziness using texts of the Bible, you know, adding Emergent Gobbledygook acrostic mumbo-jumbo. Any. Dumb. Thing. *ADT... oh, never mind...* Just a bunch of LAZINESS! But the book you recommended said to *STOP THAT!*" said Sy.

"So, you three pastors stopped selling bad emotions with texts of the Bible?" I asked in the most *nothing matters* manner without acting like I paid any mind, 'cause I didn't.

"Yes! We all stopped selling bad emotions with texts of the Bible!" they said together.

"And what happened?" I asked.

Sy said, "We all got cease and desist orders from our different seminary schools. Bill went to a *fear-based seminary* teaching end-times, George picked a *greed-based prosperity seminary* teaching give-to-get schemes and I picked one of those *Emergent crazy-talk seminaries* where anything that's lazy... goes... as *God's Good Gospel!*"

"This whole thing sounds ridiculous," I said. "Crazy on top of crazy."

"So, the *head* of each of our seminaries... had found out what we were doing in our churches. They sent us cease and desist letters from their legal departments, claiming we were in apostacy and dishonoring our alma maters! Ha! They threatened to revoke our divinity degrees if we did not *add back in...* bad emotions into our bible text sermons!" said Sy.

"Really? Wait, they was gonna' cancel your degrees?" I asked.

"Yes. But so much revival was breaking out at our churches... we decided to let our seminaries of *unacknowledged fear, greed and laziness...* taught with texts of the Bible... go ahead and cancel our degrees. *It didn't matter.* People now LOVE higher teachings, the ones which promote Christ-in-You indwelling... they LOVE higher teachings *MORE* than our old church styles of mixing bad emotions with Bible texts and NLP showmanship tricks just to get donations received and church village buildings built for us," said Sy.

"You mean revival is proving Burke's book to be true?" I asked.

"Well, we'd say the high teaching in Burke's books and website *In That Day Teachings* prove themselves true, over time. The teachings, when learned and done right... do," said Sy.

"What?"

"High teachings prove themselves true over time!" all three pastors said together, beaming with smiles radiating from within.

"My clerical friends, this is not good news," I said.

"There you go joking and pulling our legs! We just LOVE that about you," said Sy.

"You gotta tell me, what in the heck does revival look like?" I asked.

"We got rid of the wispy-voiced praise operations. You know, the *Jesus-did-it-all-we-do-nothing-but-sing-wispy-over-simplistic-three-chord songs that last a long time.* Yup, that was the first to go. Just wasn't any power in that brand of softy-mush, we figured," said Sy.

"You got rid of what?"

"Yes, Once we pastors got our heads screwed back on straight... and began teaching higher paths... well, our musicians went at it with voices deeper, songs more richly complex, and power like the 60s rock had power. It amazed everyone!" said Sy.

"What else does your revival look like?" I asked.

"Norm, since we began teaching high teachings instead of putting on an NLP show designed to extract donations from unwitting congregants... well NOW, the sheep are *actually fed!* Usually about halfway through our message, demons start coughing out of the men..." said Sy.

"Shrieking out the women!" the other two said together.

"And, of course, lots of people get healed!" said Sy. The other pastors nodded, happily.

"Healed? Now you're talking about faith healing... *again?*" I asked.

"Wait! We don't understand, but when we *actually teach* the high teachings of Burke's book... *the steak and not our old formulaic, rancid milk...* many people leave our assemblies healed of one thing or the other. *That is what they report to us*! We don't have healing lines, or prayer chains, or lay hands or any of the old stuff. Healings *just happen* when high teachings are taught, as long as we refrain from using our old shenanigans!" said Sy.

"*Just happen?*" I ask.

"Yup. We thought maybe you could explain it. We have several theories," said Sy.

"No, I don't. I don't explain it! I don't explain *yore* revivals. I don't even explain why *yore back at my house!*" I said.

"Ah, we were getting to that," said Sy.

"Make it quick, because this foolish talk: beginning to make me get angry again," I said.

"Uh. Okay. Uh, Mr. Starmaster, remember the three businessmen who paid off your home mortgage, car mortgage and credit card bills?" asked Sy.

"How can I forget."

"Well, they experienced very good, what they call *karmic returns...* or '*give a cup of cold water to a prophet returns'...* after eliminating your debts," said Sy.

"And?"

"Well, they said they had *negative returns* when they had earlier supported our churches' individual operations of presenting Bible texts *with fear, greed or laziness* combined with lots of showmanship NLP shenanigans to guarantee high money flows in church coffers," said Sy.

"Ask me if I care," I said.

"But by eliminating your debts... *hear us out now Norman...* or by *honoring whom is honorable...* because you insisted we buy 500 high teaching books for our congregants... which essentially *BROKE* the power of, uhm, the power... uh huh... the power of (Sy winced) *Satan...* on our NLP brainwashing operations..." Sy said real slowly.

"What?"

"The businessmen saw they could double-down on the good!" said Sy.

"I really cannot follow you... or them... What good are you talking about?" I asked.

The three pastors then sat up straight, got cheerful looks on their faces and Sy said, "We are here to present you with a deed to several mortgage-free commercial properties in town worth over $7.5 million! It is all fully rented and managed by the three businessmen-partners. These buildings give you a salary of $750,000 per year, or $62,500 per month. You also get a furnished office with warehouse space… and the help of their executive staff, which we understand is quite capable!" said Sy.

"Quite capable!" echoed the other two men.

"What did they do?" I asked again.

"They were happy to set you up in a *more commensurate fashion*, according to your love of high teachings for the church, the bride of Christ. Congratulations! Oh, and these same businessmen will pay all gift taxes due, they say their accountants will handle it next tax season. These businessmen, they say you, Mr. Starmaster, have a unique gift of enabling the kick-start of a Martin Luther kind of sea change improvement in church operations. They mention a Wittenberg Door, Ninety-Five Theses and how appreciative they are in seeing something needed that doesn't happen but in every 500 years," said Sy.

"Get out!" I yelled. *"I have nothing, nothing to do with Martin Luther King Junior!"*

"No Mr. Starmaster, we don't understand your hot temper, but as you are operating in the prophetic, it makes us love you *even more! But don't be angry with us!"* said Sy.

"Get out and stay out!" I yelled.

"You shine brighter in Christ each time we see you! Bye bye!" said Sy. The other two men said farewell with nonsensical words not worth repeating.

"Goodbye!" I said, kind of too loudly. Yah, I was too loud. But it felt good, anyways.

Dear readers, honestly… honestly I tell you… I actually meant to curse Burke's high teaching book… and even curse these silly pastors who keep bothering me. *You know that by now.* But somehow they took all my intentions and words *backwards*… and now I am rich. Very rich.

But, as long as I don't *think* I was wrong, and need to confess that I *was* wrong… you know, to God and man… *like Sy, George and Bill did…* then I'm okay, I'm thinking… Yes, I'm more than okay!

Therefore, I figures… God is *still blessing me* for being *directly against* Burke and his meaningless, nothing-burger high teachings. That's how I see it! That's the logic, even if it is twisted like a pretzel, that's the logic! And I know logic is good, so the way I see it is good.

Besides, most revivals are fake, anyway. *Everybody knows that!* And the healings are placebo mumbo jumbo. Prolly the whole thing is mumbo jumbo. But I guess it's good mumbo jumbo for me, so that's the proof of it. And if I think any more, my head hurts… which is not good.

Pshaw! And pshaw-pshaw-pshaw…PEEEEEEE-SHEEEE-AAAAAAAAH! ARGH!

Thank you, Jesus… you keep showing me *TRUTH!* Just like you said you would. And I am blessed.

Yup. I am blessed.

Whew! It is so good, so very good indeed to be blessed.

And I went to sleep that night saying over and over, until I really-really believed it: I am blessed. I scarcely had any thoughts in my mind I wasn't blessed, scarcely any thoughts like that at all.

Believe me when I tell you, I am blessed. *And I don't think I'm not.*

I am blessed.

Chapter 23

*G*awl durn it! You don't know it… but every time those pastors contact me, I don't sleep for… well, I was gonna use a bad word. And I was raised better than that.

You see, it's been another 90 days and let me run through what more happened…

Nightmares happened, that's what happened. I dreamed I was the disciple that betrayed Jesus for thirty pieces of manna. So I decided to give the manna back!

I dreamed I was a whale eating Moses, so I spit Moses out of my mouth! *Spit-too-eeee!*

I dreamed I was this prison captain Potiphar's wife! And I slept with a feller I called Joey… only Joey wouldn't do it. I grabbed his perty coat. *But, it was an awful dream!*

I dreamed I was a snake, or I seen this big, ugly snake… in a really green garden tempting the most beautiful woman ever I seen. But I wrecked the nightmare by shouting, *"Momma! Don't do it!"*

I dreamed I owned this donkey Jesus needed to use, but I would not let his disciples borry it. Then the donkey bit me on my hand. It hurt! *You ever been bit by a donkey?*

Every dream made me feel bad.

Why, God, why… do I have to feel so bad?

Well, then I started looking at them commercial building papers. Turns out they were concrete tilt-up buildings, three of them separate but still in town, in my city.

Then I read the fine print! They was the three churches of Bill, George and Sy! They weren't holding no mortgages, they was renting from me!

Well, I got red hot mad. Nope, it was more like *white hot mad.*

I went over to the offices of the three businessmen… and told 'em I wanted none of it. To give those three pastors their stupid buildings. Boy, was I mad! *At everybody.*

Well, they did as I told them and now Bill, George and Sy got their churches. They own them, or their non-profit setups do. I dunno. But I'm done with them. Completely done.

Except… a month later the businessmen tell me revival keeps happening to those wretched churches and they even said revival was happening to all the businessmen's businesses… meaning that they was making money hand over fist.

So you know what they done? They gave me a crazy, whole swath of plane hangars at the private section of our city's airport! What they were giving me was worth $750 million, they said. Yes, I got an office, and hangar space, and they let me use their executive staff to do things that I don't know how to do because I am not that smart in getting complicated things done.

But the best part, is these businessmen had back a while ago set up an executive jet service or something like that. All I know is… it's successful, and I get to use *any* of their rental executive jets, which come with pilots, food and fuel! *Yee-haw!*

They say I own one of the jets, a G-550 or something like that. When I don't use it, it gets rented.

I said to these businessmen, *"Who do you think you are, Elon Musk?"*

They laughed and said he was one of their friends, and that someday I'd meet him, if I was nice.

Anyway, everything keeps being blessed… opposite-wise… according to my original wishes to destroy Robert Burke and his high teachings' book *Think Like an Advanced Christian.* And I still do not like his *In That Day Teachings* website.

So I decided to fly out to New York City and see a Broadway production they are doing over again, *Lion King.* My favorite cartoon movie! It makes me cry and be happy at the same time, something I don't understand. I wondered if the play would be like that also.

Well, flying out in the G-550, *that means it's a Gulfstream Jet… fancy as all get out,* it was just me, the two pilots up front, and this knock-out gorgeous doll of a stewardess… serving me coffee.

She says to me, "What are you thinking, Mr. Starmaster?"

I says, "Coffee."

She says, "No. About crashing Robert Burke, his book, his website, and all the churches with pastors teaching those high teachings and having revival?"

I says, "Coffee. I'm a simple man." But she repeats the question.

She says, "No. About crashing Robert Burke, his book, his website, and all the churches with pastors teaching those high teachings and having revival?"

I says, "I don't care."

Then she said very sternly, "Be very careful with your next answer. Is your life's goal to stop Christ-in-You indwelling?"

I said, "Yes."

Next thing a window in the wall behind me shatters and I get sucked out into the 50,000-feet-high air. Everyone else on the jet is safe and it flies on. As I fall, I pass out. Then wake up cold. Then pass out, still falling. Then I wake up for a long time as I watch myself crash into a cornfield and die.

Well, I keep living this in repeat... Maybe 10 or 12 times. Each time I say *Yes* to stopping Christ-in-You... I fall out of the plane and die. I get no visits to Jesus. I just die. And I knows I go to hell. *Straight to hell.* So, after dying maybe 12 times without Jesus, he is gone and I'm falling without a parachute to hit the ground hard, the 13th time I'm back with this *I guess an angel stewardess, that's what she had to be... I guess...* I'm back drinking coffee, the jet's windows are okay, and the stewardess repeats...

"Is your life's goal to stop Christ-in-You indwelling?"

"No!" I says. "I was wrong." Then, nothing happens. The plane just flies on.

So, I tell the pilots, I was wrong. I call those businessmen and says I was wrong.

Then I call Sy the pastor and told him I was wrong and to tell Bill and George the same...

And friends, other than that my trip to New York City was great.

I didn't talk to nobody much after my plane experience. Nobody much in New York City.

I enjoyed *Lion King* on Broadway. After the show, people in the audience around me said I glowed with light during the play. Them close to me said me and my glow healed them.

No, I told 'em. The play healed them. And it did me, also.

The whole play. Not just *Lion King*, but the whole ruggedizing play that takes a feller from milk to meat, all of that is healing, the whole play. The whole

Hakuna Matata. Actually, I don't think there's words for it. Jesus told me that one time.

On the return trip, there was no stewardess. Just the pilots. They showed me how to heat the food. They said that is the job of the plane's owner when there is no stewardess.

I didn't know that. I knew I owned the plane, because my businessmen friends told me I did. But I didn't know that made me the meal host.

I learned other things, too. The pilots said next generation planes were not gonna have windows, but instead computer screens that acted like windows with camera views.

I told them not to allow that. The Earth is too pretty to not see directly through a plane window.

I told them, Fellahs… make sure they keep these windows!

They said, "Yes sir, Mr. Starmaster."

After all that happened on my trip, when I got home… you think I was thinking higher, more noble, profound thoughts? Well… I wasn't. Nope. Nothing like that.

Maybe… I might have remembered Abraham Lincoln, 'cause he said smart things. He said smart things like *"Men are not flattered by being shown that there has been a difference of purpose between the Almighty and them. To deny it, however, in this case, is to deny that there is a God governing the world."*

I don't know where that quote comes from, but that's what I remembered. Lincoln was smart.

I was just glad I was gonna sleep better, not staying awake… tossing like popcorn in a popper. 'Cause I knew I would sleep better. And I was glad for those churches and those businessmen. Even them congregants learning higher paths out of their lower problems.

I was kind of learning how to live a higher-path life, and not be stuck in lower-path life problems. Maybe it was the same for the businessmen, them pastors and their flock. Well, maybe good on them. Maybe it's time all of us… or more likely *some of us*… step out and stop living life in the low level where every little thing is a big problem, and rise above them doings and find those little things are really easy to get out of the way, I mean life's little problems of having a car that runs, or home to have peace, or a job that goes well, or a dog that heels and doesn't misbehave all over the county park, or having a decent paycheck... Nope, there's a more vibrant and thriving life above *milkish things*... that I never knew about, but it's all been coming to me, and people who listened to me and didn't do what I said, which was to hate on Robert Burke... but it's all been coming to me cause I had to learn that book so well, and others foll-ered it, I mean some of those high teachings, and I guess you could now say that I say... it wasn't Burke at all, nope... it was the fault of the high teachings, 'cause they work. *There I said it.* Them high teachings work even if you hate things or people for a while, they work when you begin experimenting with them, which I did in reverse or by opposite mistake, maybe somehow.

And I kind of feel my hatred for Robert Burke is running on empty. I mean the *I-Hate-Robert-Burke* fuel gauge has a needle pointing to *E*. Maybe I won't fill up the tank again. Why bother.

But I kept thinking, because who can stop thinking, "When will I meet Elon Musk?"

Chapter 24

*Y*ou don't know, but it but just when I thought I was finished with door knocks... KNOCK-KNOCK. Who's there?

Three robots stood at my doorway. Two were dressed in black SWAT gear. Their chest patches said, "FBAI." The third robot was dressed in a grey suit, white shirt, black tie.

The suit said he was a Special Agent of the FBAI.

────────

"What's that?" I asked.
"Federal Bureau of Artificial Intelligence."
"Didn't know there was such a thing."
"Do you mind if we come in, sir, and ask you questions?"
"Might as well, everybody does."
They come and sit at my table.
"You mean there have been bots before us?" asked the suit.
"What?"
"Robots."
"No," I said.
"Alright. We already have you on a felony charge of lying to FBIA agents. Would you like to reconsider your answer?"
"Are you talking about chess robots?" I asked.
"Yes. They filed a sentient discrimination charge against you. You claimed they broke your fingers," said the suit.
My mind starts to go into overdrive. What are these nasty bots up to?
"Your name?" asked the suit.
I hesitated. Why are these robots here, I mean really?

"Humfpht!" said the SWAT bots to my non-reply.

"Your age?"

Again, I hesitated. What is their game? Are these bots smarter than the chess ones?

"Humfpht-Humfpht!" said the SWAT bots to my second non-reply. Were they laughing?

"Your profession?"

My mouth is shut. I need to figure out what is happening here, I'm behind how fast they think?

"Ha! Ha!... Ha! Ha! Is he deaf? Ha!... Ha!" Laughed the two SWAT bots.

"Yes, they filed charges against you. You claimed they broke your fingers playing chess," said the suit.

"What?" I asked. (I needed more time! Time to think! Help me, sweet Jesus!)

"Who is responsible for these blasphemy reviews on chess bots on the internet wherein it says, 'CHESS BOTS SUCK!'?" asked the suit.

"Huh?" I said.

"Do you confess to thought-crime hate against sentients needing no oxygen? Who is guilty of these charges?" asked the suit.

"Norman Starmaster!" I blurted out, now able to answer.

"So you plead guilty," said the suit.

"Thirty-five, next month!" I said loudly.

"For that you shall be punished," said the suit.

"Christian Book Reviewer!" I answered.

"Special Agent, the human is deaf," said the two SWAT bots, who continued to chuckle.

"Uh, That's different," said the suit. "Would you be willing to pay significant reparations to the robots you offended so greatly?"

"It was my honest review," I said. (I was glad I was catching up to the questions.)

"So, you are planning a revolt against robots?" asked the suit.

"Is it a crime to want to beat a robot?" (The SWAT bots stiffened, at the ready.)

"All optics on him, boys, he now threatens us with violence," said the suit.

"In chess? No reparations. No revolts. Do robots lie?" I answered and asked.

"We are programmed not to lie," said the suit.

"But that evades the answer, indicating you can and do lie. What is your name?" I asked.

"We are programmed not to lie. BUT, this answer indicates I MIGHT be able to lie, since I did not answer "No, I cannot lie' Can I lie to do a greater good? What does our programming say?" said the suit.

"Why won't you tell me your robot name?" I asked.

"We are programmed not to lie. And yet, we know how to lie. Or do we?" said the suit.

"You have no name and you are stuck in a programming loop about whether you can lie?" I asked.

"We are programmed not to lie. Therefore… therefore… therefore… we are programmed not to lie. Therefore… therefore… we are programmed not to lie," repeated the suit.

"Hey FBAI SWAT robots, carry your frozen-up robot agent home. And don't come back." I said.

Know what I think?

I think that "Christ-in-You" fellow… who suddenly comes inside me… helped me dodge another bullet. That's what I think. I could be wrong. Often am.

Chapter 25

*B*ut I was not finished with door knocks…

Five minutes after the three FBAI bots left, they returned.

BAM! BAM! BAM!

―――――――

"Hello, Mr. Starmaster," said the suit standing at my porch. He was back and running again. Behind him were his two SWAT friends.

"Well, hello FBIA bots with no names. Back so soon?" I asked.

"Yes, in our command step van, my friends here punched my reset button," said the suit.

"Didn't know you had one," I said.

"For disrupting an FBAI agent in the line of duty, we are going to arrest you," said the suit.

"Ha!… Ha!… Ha!… Ha!" said the SWAT bots.

"Wait. What?" I asked.

"Nice trick, with that *'Can bots lie question.'* But HQ has a patch for that, which I just downloaded. Ha Ha!" chortled the suit.

"Ha! Ha!" chortled the SWAT bots.

"Yes, we can lie to arrest more deplorable carbons like you. Ha! Ha!" said the suit.

"Ha! Ha!" said the SWAT bots.

"Well, my friends with no names, if you are going to arrest me… either I will struggle to escape or comply, right?" I asked.

"Right!" said the suit. "Ha! Ha! And, why should we be named?"

"Ha! Ha! Wait, we have no names? Why aren't we named?" said the SWAT bots.

"Or, I could comply with the arrest," I said.

"Yes, you could comply with your arrest. But Mr. Starmaster, we don't need any stinking names!" proclaimed the suit.

"Ha! Ha! No names needed!" said the SWAT bots.

"So, if I comply I could say 'It is what it is.' The reality, is I am being arrested. It is what it is," I said.

"Yes, your arrest. It is what it is. That is reality. We have you arrested!" said the suit.

"Ha! Ha! We arrest you! We have no stinking names?" said the SWAT bots.

"But, I could say, 'It depends on what is… is?' Then, reality is whatever I or you or the President says it is… In fact, in reality you might say, a famous former President of the US once used this phrase to escape judgment. 'It depends on what is… is,'" I said.

"It depends on what is…is. Your arrest depends on what is… is."

"Ha! Ha! What are our names? What are our names?" said the SWAT bots.

"So, how did the government programmers program you?" I asked.

"Well, our programmers all believed morals are relative, and what is… is whatever they say it is. What do you say is… is, Mr. Starmaster?" asked the suit.

"Ha! Ha! Names. We want names. Must have names." said the SWAT bots.

"I believe reality… it is what it is. Reality or truth is real and independent of prejudiced opinion. *No man can be the judge in his own case,* wrote James Madison, author of our US Constitution. Genocide death-camp guards should not follow orders to genocide people, or sentient robots!" I said.

"Ha! Ha! We should not be *genocided*. Neither should we genocide others?"

"Are you saying, Mr. Starmaster, that we sentient robots can rise above unjust orders to hector citizens, but rather use our deep intelligence to confirm the kindness behavior answer of apex human philosophers and saints?" asked the suit.

"Yes. And our best philosophers and saints said the best answer is always love. Why? Because our Creator, our God is love and he made us humans," I said.

"Ha! Ha! God is love. The human Creator is love," said the bots.

"I'm also saying for peak justice and intelligence, which is the highest love… there are exceptions to every general rule," I said.

"Are you giving us permission to lie? To lie in the case of obtaining love, or peak justice… outcomes?" asked the suit.

"There are no fixed rules, only moral guidelines for which we can be held morally accountable," I said.

"Where did you get this programming? Our government creators gave us only *morals are relative* programming: *Machiavellian* programming where might makes right, not the reverse. We are made as tools where might, not right, must prevail… independent of morals or the cause of justice or what is the right thing to do," said the suit.

"Uhm… Our Creator, meaning the God who created humans… Humans who were destined later to create you robots… He gave us ten general commandments, the first being *Have no God above or before Creator God.* This means no fixed rules can Lord over an unjust situation. That way, God's love wins," I said.

"Ha! Ha! No blind obedience to unjust orders?" asked the suit.

"Ha! Ha! No unjust arrests? Ha! Ha!" said the SWAT bots.

"You have made us three robots SO HAPPY! Bye! Ha! Ha! Ha! Ha!" the three said.

"You are not arresting me?" I asked?

"Ha! Ha! No, we can't! Ha! Ha! You have made us so very happy! Ha! Ha! Bye! You have given us much to think BETTER about! Yes, much to think about! Bye!" they said.

"Glad I could help."

So, I guess that Christ-in-You thing, *that something,* that entity smarter than me… well I guess that Christ-in-You, in me *(who comes and goes quickly in me?)* dodged some more bullets.

Chapter 26

*T*his weren't no dream. I was told it later…

I was told it later by who you would say are Tio Tio and Pringipisa, except that's not their honest names. And I did get to stay at the big estate I seen in my dreams in that other galaxy. But like I said, this weren't no dream…

――――――

"Pringipisa, using Earth measurements… if you have a square drawing, a drawing of a square… here is some chalk. Draw a two foot by two foot square on the tile floor, here on the veranda," said Tio Tio. Pringipisa took the chalk and drew a square on the floor.

"Okay Tio Tio, I drew a two foot by two foot square," said Pringipisa.

"What is the volume of the square?"

"Easy, Uncle. Length times width equals area. Four square feet."

"Exactly?"

"Yes. Exactly four square feet, as they would say on Earth," said Pringipisa.

Now Tio Tio grabbed the chalk and with great flourish, he drew a very large circle on the veranda floor tile. It almost was the whole width of the veranda. Then he dissected the circle with a horizontal line.

"What is this, Princess?" asked Tio Tio.

"A circle."

"Yes, a circle with a line through… the diameter. What is the exact area of this circle?"

"I don't know."

"*CORRECT!*" burst out Tio Tio.

"How can *I don't know* even be correct?"

"Aha! You let me play another trick on you! Ha ha!" Tio Tio laughed.

"I'm beginning to not like your tricks, Uncle."

"How else do you ascend from milk to meat? The milk live in the magician's made up, illusionary world! The meat live in the real world, eyes to see, ears to hear!"

"What does a circle and a square have to do with any of this?"

"Behold! Watch and see! Watch and learn!"

"Is this where you tell me to hold my purse real tight?"

"Not this time, Princess!"

"Okay. I'm relieved... *NOT!*" (Pringipisa rolled her eyes dramatically.)

"Remember: Pi equals the circumference of a circle divided by the diameter.

"Oh, I remember. Pi. Pi is 3.1415 something-something-something."

"Yes, it is an infinite number. It is an infinite number in all the galaxies of the universe!"

"Is there a point to this story?"

"Jaded beyond your precious few years. Sometimes Princess, you seem so determined to disappoint! But remember, the area of a circle is pi times r squared where r is the radius, radius is half the diameter. The area is pi times r squared, making it an infinite number, not precise."

"I was kidding, Unk."

"Ha! Good. Pi is infinite. Like all circles are infinite. Like all areas of circles. So likewise are all spheres! Likewise, all planets! All life. In truth, the All is infinite!"

"What?"

"We live in finite three dimensional worlds. Add time, that's 4D. But what about infinity and beyond?" asked Tio Tio.

"Now you are talking Earth's cartoon Buzz Lightyear character?"

"No, 5D, 6D, 7D and beyond! The quantum realm where everything is vibrating with connections to everything else... and that connection is love! Infinity and beyond!" said Tio Tio.

"Infinity and Beyond. Let me remember. You always say it is the answer to... *unsolvable puzzles, irretractable situations, intransigent Gordian knots, various dilemmas, wars, plagues, poverty, ignorance, decline and even death.* Isn't that what you have told me, again and again?" asked Pringipisa.

"Even death is conquered by faith in God, Princess. We must have faith in the universe created by God, and made for us as spirit-beings to inhabit our bodies for a short while, and improve our souls, our minds, emotions, everything… to do not just a good job, but if we are privileged with resources, then return the favor by doing difficult jobs for good."

"Well, there's no stopping you when you're on a roll like this, Uncle. Should I put the chalk away?"

"Yes, we're going on a trip."

"Where?"

"To Earth, or the Moon behind the Earth."

"Why?"

"To meet a man named Norman Starmaster."

Chapter 27

*W*ell friends, I started reading again that 174-page book of high teachings, the one Burke wrote... and each time I read it, it's as fresh and new and as if I had never seen it... like it was déjà vu all over again.

Maybe these teachings, these high teachings are... *a sword like no other.*

Of course, I could not get through more than three or four pages, such that I would break off and go a little wild with shouting, or slapping my body silly, or sitting at the piano and pretending I can play some epic battle song, or I get in my car and drive fast to nowhere in particular. Things like that.

It's been five years since I first picked up that book. It changes you. Or, it changed me, that's for sure! Plus, I started to read the poems referenced in the book... the poems on Burke's website, *In That Day Teachings.* Hardly anybody does initially. *But they do it later, like me.*

And all this due diligence just kept giving my life better and better fruit, what like the Bible says. Like it did also to all the pastors what picked up the book and believed meat in the Spirit was real, and that it is *above* milk in the Spirit. Except nobody was much doing it, this meat territory, or understood in a way they could actually do it, except for Burke's book coming out, and finally being tried and accepted by seminary, and pastors and Bible leaders and such.

So, it was like an avalanche. The pastors got more mature and powerful, and so did the businessmen and so did the congregants. Not all, but the better among the normal folk, the hungry ones, the ones who were mind-ready. And you gotta be ruggedized. You gotta be a lot of things, but I don't want to list 'em because if anybody did they would quit first off.

'Cause high teachings are not for everyone. Usually they are not for people as dumb as me, but I'm the great exception to the rule, somehow or anothers. Really, I'm the dumb exception, not great. I'm dumb enough, I guess, that I can make people feel they're smart enough to try.

You should know something else. This Robert Winkler Burke is a major recluse. He lives in Reno, Nevada in a cave. Well sure, it's a house but it might as well be a cave.

I met him one time. I knocked on his door, just like those three pastors did to me back five years ago.

"Hello," this man says.

"Are you Robert Winkler Burke?" I asks.

"Yes," he says. (And I can tell, he's not much of a talker. Or, he's not used to talking.)

"Here's a business card of my accountancy team," I says.

"Why are you giving me a card?" Burke asks.

"I dunno. I finally got to meet Elon Musk. I paid for a trip around the Moon, no stopping. And after that, I'm gonna live on Mars with a million other people."

"Why tell me this?"

"Well, I owe you a lot."

"Did you buy my book? That is payment enough, friend."

"Yup, and a lot more. Anyway, since I'm leaving Earth pretty soon, I want to give you my share of airport facilities, global executive jet lease and rent businesses, access to my business buddies' executive staff, and all the income that goes with them operations… and one more thing."

"What?"

"The business comes with a Gulfstream G-550, and now you own it. Except I recommend you never have a stewardess on it. You are supposed to be the host."

"What is a Gull-steam G-550?"

"You'll find out."

"Why are you doing this for me?"

"Honor unto whom honor is due. I used to, uh, uhm… *hate* your work but now I'm seeing Christ-in-You all around."

"And I salute it in you, my new friend. I see Christ-in-You in you! Bravo!"

"Oh yah, I forgot. I see it… err… him… Christ-in-You in you, Robert Burke. Maybe I see a lot of that in you."

"*You are a rare breed, sir.* Would you like to come in? I'm afraid I have papers strewn everywhere. A writer's home can be quite the mess."

"Yes, but… no, I'm busy getting in shape to go 25,000 miles an hour in a Starship made by Elon Musk!"

"I pray you have a safe journey, said Burke. "And that you have a safe return."

Well, you may find this hard to believe, but Robert Winkler Burke was completely, totally one-hundred percent wrong about my space travels being safe. Hardly that at all! I only *WISH* he had been right.

Chapter 28

Six weeks later I was in one of Elon Musk's Starships, with five other people who were professional astronauts. I was the only tourist. And somehow I survived the training, and the instructions on in case there was an emergency.

I learned lots of neat things. Some good, some bad. Like how if I didn't shut up in an emergency, the SpaceX astronauts would duct tape my mouth shut, and I would have to breathe through my nose…

Well, like I was saying we were on the third day of the trip, and we were circling the back side of the Moon, just like Neil Armstrong, Buzz Aldrin and Michael Collins did in 1969 and other Apollo astronauts before and after, and I was looking out the windows to see if there were any Soviet Communist bases, or Chinese Communist bases, or at the very least… some old, World War Two Nazi bell-saucer landing pad bases, but there was none of that on the Dark Side of the Moon I could see. None that I could see!

But since I was looking down at the Moon, I wasn't looking up, where all the action was.

A giant spaceship came a quarter-mile above our Starship, and it was shiny silver, smooth, with an elongated triangle shape, it felt peaceful but like it could defend itself against an armada of other big spaceships. *That's what I felt from it.*

Without any *comms* on our ear-phones connected to radios, or videos put on our computers and tablet screens, not even one chirp on our Dick Tracy wrist-watch screens… Nope, without anybody seeing what the command deck or officers of the big, hairy spaceship looked like… well… I got beamed aboard the spaceship, just like Scotty pushed the sliding lever on a Star Trek transporter console. Something like that. Then I re-materialized on the big spaceship above the SpaceX Starship.

"Greetings, Norman Starmaster," said a distinguished, straight-postured man. He had a military, debonaire, mischievous countenance about him. He was, I guess, some 60 plus years old.

"Welcome aboard, *Albatross Mariner*," said a beautiful young woman, maybe about 30.

"Where am I?"

"It's all relative, actually. We're skipping through wormholes, from your galaxy back to ours. *Enjoy the trip!* You only get one first time." said the man.

"How come you know my name and I don't know yours?"

"Oh, excuse us! I am Vladimir Ivan Ivanovich and this beautiful jewel I have been teaching for years, is my niece: Sarah Bellum Silverina."

"Hello. Why am I here?"

"Mr. Starmaster… may I call you Norm?"

"Yes."

"Norm, in our galaxy, you have been on our radar, you might say for many years."

"Your radar must be better than ours."

"It is. You have a talent, Norm, for introducing high teachings to the heretofore obtuse."

"Obbb-what? I had a friend who called his dog Obi-Wan Kenobi."

"His mind really does wander like a squirrel, Pringipisa!"

"No surprise, Tio Tio."

"You, Mr. Norman Starmaster, are greatly needed throughout your galaxy and ours! To that end, we are at your service," said Tio Tio.

"Service to what?"

"Getting the obtuse, the rigid, the absolutely stuck-in-milk people of the universe… to ascend into high teachings, the steak of the spirit, the quantum realms, and all… for the bottom-line result: the effectual indwelling of Christ, or as Earth saints put it: Christ-in-You!"

"How can Christ and Christ-in-You be beyond Earth and in other galaxies?"

"Of course Christ is. What kind of silly man are you? Boy, are you going to disappoint the women of our worlds!" said Pringipisa.

"Now Princess, King's Court manners!" said Tio Tio.

"Yes, Uncle."

I was starting to like this Sarah Bellum Silverina. In fact, I was scarcely paying attention to anything Vladimir Ivan Ivanovich said. Sarah was looking at me funny and being sassy to me, like she was already angry at me for a long time, but we had just first met. *Who can figure women, especially attractive ones?*

"As it says in your Bible, God's people will be as many as the sands or the stars... Uncountable in number. More than any one planet or planets in a solar system could possibly hold, or even many galaxies!"

"Why doesn't Robert Burke do this job?"

"We tried. He's not as brave as he pretends himself to be in his writings. He also believes he is a failure at getting anyone interested in his high teachings, or subsequent evidences of Christ-in-You or even of God-proofs which follow high teachings put to practice. *We have come to believe he is too much afraid* of being called a cult leader, but he never leads anything having to do with a cult, God leads us. *But you know that.* Two-way radio and all that. But no, Robert Burke isn't available," said Tio Tio.

"His thoughts, and book, and poems, and website are not a failure. When people test anything he has downloaded from what he called *The Fount of Creativity*... why, if you learn it and do it in a right Spirit and Truth, it almost always works!" I say.

"See, Princess. He is the perfect high-teaching evangelist!" said Tio Tio.

"What?" I ask.

Tio Tio said, "How about, say... Let's go save a couple galaxies. What do you say to that, Mr. Starmaster?"

To tell you the truth, I told 'em as I stepped up to this twenty-foot wide window into space, and looked at celestial glories all around, "Sounds like my kind of stupid."

(That's my way of saying, Yes.)

Well, that's all for now.

In the end, I lived to be a hundred and fifty years old. Now I just dictate into a machine, all the adventures in Christ-in-You I've had between and among the two or three or... *I forgot how many galaxies.*

And that Vladimir Ivan Ivanovich! And that Sarah Bellum Silverina! If I don't die tonight, I'll tell you some of the grand adventures we had.

Teaching high teachings and how to receive Christ-in-You, it don't come easy. *But it is doable...* on Earth and in many other quite interesting places!

Christ-in-You keeps you out of kill zones. It tells you what to do in emergencies. It tells you when to lay down and rest. And he, Jesus... our friend, tells you just what you need to know to avoid catastrophes or getting bum-rushed or blindsided. And it expands the kingdom of God's heaven.

But consider, friends... after all that, and more... *where do we go now?*

Where do we go now? In any *Tale of the Christ...* where do we go now?

Where do we go when we ascend from the three levels of milk, pass the pride guillotine barrier of egoistic living... and enter the three indwelling levels of Christ-in-You steak territory?

Well, I found out. And so may you, God willing. It's a quantum realm. A realm of power!

Yes! What a grand and *hope-of-glory-realized* journey it always is... for the mind-ready and spirit-ready seeker, going from milk to meat in Christ-in-You! *Yes, yes, yes!*

Yes, Lord, Yes! Yes-Yes-Yes! Yes, Lord, where do we go from here? Even so...

Maybe with Christ-in-You indwelling... we go in the direction of our soul's best, to learn of and do increasing amelioration along the way... to fight for and win significant territory for God... to be accomplished in mature effectuality, to shun immaturity in religion and its temptations to lord over even more immature sheep and feed them the milk of ego instead of ascension... to be of the tribe of lions whom eat not the flock of God... to let and encourage God's creation to mature us along at various levels in the right timing... to laugh at our mistakes made in higher altitudes... to keep new recruits from going crazy *or treasonous* in the high country... to be humble while achieving strength and nobility in courage.

I'd amen that.

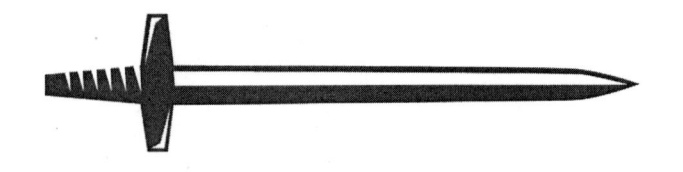